THEY CALL ME THE MERCENARY

#6

VENGEANCE ARMY

Books by Jerry Ahern

The Survivalist Series
#1: Total War
#2: The Nightmare Begins
#3: The Quest
#4: The Doomsayer
#5: The Web
#6: The Savage Horde
#7: The Prophet
#8: The End is Coming
#9: Earth Fire
#10: The Awakening

The Defender Series
#1: The Battle Begins
#2: The Killing Wedge
#3: Out of Control
#4: Decision Time
#5: Entrapment

They Call Me the Mercenary Series
#1: The Killer Genesis
#2: The Slaughter Run
#3: Fourth Reich Death Squad
#4: The Opium Hunter
#5: Canadian Killing Ground
#6: Vengeance Army

THEY CALL ME THE MERCENARY

#6

VENGEANCE ARMY

JERRY AHERN

SPEAKING VOLUMES, LLC

NAPLES, FLORIDA

2012

THEY CALL ME THE MERCENARY

VENGEANCE ARMY #6

ISBN 978-1-61232-215-5

For Jerry Rakusan, a hell of an editor in the gun

magazine business, a good friend and teacher—and

one fine man carrying a heavy load.

Chapter One

Hank Frost looked in the refrigerator. One of the disadvantages, he decided, of almost never living in your apartment was that you always ran out of things. He glanced at the Omega Seamaster 120 on his left wrist. It was seven-thirty A.M. and a Sunday morning at that. "The hell with it," he said out loud, then, slamming the refrigerator door walked out of the small kitchen and across the empty living room, past the black and white portable he'd bought back in 1969 for the Moon landing and into the bedroom.

He looked in the closet, didn't see any shirts and went to the dresser drawer. There was an old, comfortable Hathaway black knit shirt and he pulled it out of the drawer and pulled it over his head, pushing the long sleeves up past his elbows. He found his Levis and didn't bother with underpants, just stepped into them and zipped them, cursing softly as he caught the zipper on the hairs at his crotch. He found his trackshoes, pulled them on without untying them or retying them.

Frost looked at himself in the mirror, then fished in the little wooden box on the top of the dresser and took out a new eyepatch, throwing the paper that he crumpled in his fist into the wastebasket but missing. He bent over and picked it up, then put the new black patch in place over his left eye.

He snatched the Metalifed Browning High Power from the top of the dresser and dumped it under his shirt inside the waistband of his trousers slightly behind the left hip bone. He grabbed up his keys and his wallet and his money and stuffed the things into his pockets as he started for the living room again. He stopped by the door and turned around and looked at the one item of decoration in the room—an eight by ten color glossy of Bess in an easel style frame. He smiled, automatically blowing her a kiss, then reminding himself to call her again in London. The last operation on the hip would take place soon and he wanted to talk to her first—reassure her it would be all right and despite the outcome she'd be the same to him. She'd gotten shot up in Canada with Frost, and the bullet in the hip had required two operations so far—this one was to do the trick.

He grabbed his leather jacket from the hall tree in the living room and let himself out and into the corridor of the new building, bypassing the elevator and walking down two flights to the main floor and pushing through the glass doors and out into the South Bend morning—he snapped up his collar, cold with the wind blowing off the Lake the other side of the Interstate, not too many miles away. As he started walking, he wished he'd bothered with underpants because his rear end was cold.

"Milk," he muttered, trying to remember if he needed another carton of Camels. "Ahh, what the hell," he said again to himself. "I'd walk a mile—" He stopped, looking up and down the deserted street. It was too quiet. Light snow was falling and that cushioned noise but still, Frost thought. He edged his right hand under the jacket and inside his shirt and touched the Pachmayr gripped butt of the Browning for reassurance.

"Gettin' old," he muttered, then kept walking, the snow edging up inside his track shoes. Frost could see the convenience store at the end of the block and aimed toward it, rubbing his salt and pepper stubbled face with his right hand, remembering he'd forgotten his cigarettes. He hated working for Diablo Protection, he decided. There was almost always nothing to do on weekends and Sunday was the worst time, in the mornings. The convenience store was a half block away now and he tried remembering if there were anything else he needed—there were plenty of frozen pizzas, macaroni and cheese dinners. He had enough breakfast cereal and coffee and tea.

Frost kept walking.

He stopped again as he entered the parking lot, standing there a moment, watching the one set of tire tracks leading into the store's lot, the automobile parked near the door and melted snow on its hood. The quiet was still making him edgy. Frost started across the lot, his feet wet through now, the lot slippery under the mottled soles of the track shoes.

He stepped up onto the small concrete walk and approached the double glass doors. Frost turned, thinking he heard something behind him—the sixth sense again, or perhaps years of experience and five senses working into a refinement and attunement that didn't mesh in the average person, someone unaccustomed to a constant diet of life threatening situations. Frost glanced around the parking lot and saw nothing. Mentally and physically shrugging, trying to remember if there were anything else he needed besides the milk—he'd decided on a carton of cigarettes—he put his right hand on the aluminum door handle and pulled the glass door outward toward him and stepped inside.

"The floor's slippery, Mr. Frost!"

It was Jim Richards, the manager. Frost started to nod, look down to the floor. Brown slush was accumulated by it. Frost took a step and felt himself starting to go. The damned track shoes, he thought, starting to go down, trying to catch himself.

10

As he fell back, his rear end squishing hard against the wet floor, there was a blasting sound, the glass from the double doors shattering over his head, Jim Richards shouting, screaming almost, shards of plate glass spraying through the air, the front of the checkout counter suddenly perforated with what looked to Frost like dozens of holes.

Frost rolled, snatching with his mud wetted right hand for the Browning High Power in the trouser band of his jeans, snatching the rubber grips tight into his fist, his right thumb jacking back the Browning's hammer to full stand, the rest of the glass doors shattering as there was another blast, then another.

"Riot shotgun," Frost rasped to himself, then shouted to Richards, "Get down!"

Frost wanted to fire the High Power, but as yet he couldn't see any target beyond the doors, each time he looked up more of the glass shattering and his left hand going up to cover his face and his good eye. A one-eyed man's greatest fear Frost felt deep in his churning guts, was the loss of his other eye—total blindness. Frost, on his knees and elbows in the muck and glass on the floor, started to his right, down the aisle closest to the windows. Frost hit the portion of wall just below the glass and the plate glass window above him shattered, showering him with tiny, razor edged shards of glass, his hair, his hands, his neck, his face—cut and bleeding. The shotgunner was working fast now and as Frost edged along the meager protection of the wall beneath

11

the windows, the rest of the windows in the store front started shattering. Potato chips, pop bottles and cans littered the floor around him, some of the bottles smashed and the soda pop trickling across the floor into the ooze of the mud, some of the pop cans exploding as the shotgun pellets impacted against them. Keeping his head down, Frost made the decision—the car in the lot—the shotgun was there.

Frost reached up the High Power as another blast from the shotgun ripped into a rack of pickle jars, the glass exploding, pickles and vinegar spraying across the floor and all over him. Frost fired the High Power, twice, then ducked down again. There was another shotgun blast. Frost looked across the floor of the store, spotting a huge box of disposable diapers. He grabbed at it, keeping the box over his back and shoulders and neck as the shotgunner fired again, more of the glass shattering over him.

Frost reached across the aisle, grabbing a can of pork and beans, then hurtling it like a grenade through the shot-out window over his head. He grabbed another can, then another, throwing the cans out toward the car and where the shotgunner had to be.

He grabbed two cans, waited for another shotgun blast, then threw them out, firing the Browning after them. The shotgunner was still firing, Frost finding a case of unbroken pop bottles on the floor to his left, reaching out, grabbing the first bottle, shaking it hard and lobbing it like a Molotov through the window space into the parking lot.

There was a shattering of glass and Frost grabbed three more bottles, throwing them one after the other, the shotgunner firing, Frost edging up, squinting between the window ledge and the box of disposable diapers, punching the Browning's muzzle against a jagged triangle of glass, the glass shattering outward, the Browning bucking twice as Frost fired a burst toward the rear of the automobile. Hurling another of the glass pop bottles, Frost pushed himself up, flipping the window ledge, going into a roll in the snow, cutting his hands and arms on the jagged glass from the broken bottles.

Then Frost saw him, the shotgunner standing up from behind the rear deck of the automobile, footprints in the snow leading from the hedgerow near the street to the car, the pump shotgun in the man's hands firing, the shotshell pellet column lacerating the sidewalk next to Frost's left arm.

The shotgunner was tromboning the slide on the pumpgun as Frost, propped on his left elbow, legs splayed out for balance, punched the Metalifed High Power—it was sticky from the soda pop—forward and fired, once, then twice, then a third round, the first of the 115-grain gilding metal jacketed hollow points impacting into the shotgunner's chest, knocking him back on his feet, the second round making a half-dollar sized circle of blood in the center of the man's adam's apple. As blood already started spilling like vomit from the assassin's mouth, the third slug punched in at the bridge of the shotgunner's nose. The upward angle of the last shot pushed the bullet high into the cranial cavity, Frost guessed, the top of the head exploding in a mass of pink and red as the shotgun slipped from the lifeless fingers, the assassin spread-eagling back across the trunk lid of the snow littered car.

The pistol in his right hand, maybe a half magazine left, Frost judged, he pushed himself up on his bleeding left hand to his feet, side-stepping a three-inch knife edge of a pop bottle propped up like a punji stick beside his feet. He started across the lot, slowly trying to dust the glass from his hair and face, watching the mess of the shotgunner and scanning the parking lot to see if he'd had any friends. There were sirens now starting to well up over the silence of the snowy Sunday morning. Frost wheeled as he heard glass crunching behind him, holding himself from firing as he spotted Jim Richards coming through the shattered doorway. "Hey, Jim," Frost began. "When the cops and the emergency people get through, don't let me forget—I need a gallon of milk." Richard's eyes widened perceptibly. Frost shrugged, smiling, a shard of glass tinkling to the ground from his back. "I hate breakfast cereal when it's dry," Frost added lamely.

Chapter Two

Frost leaned back, naked under the sheet on the emergency room operating table, naked except for the two dozen or so bandaids on his face and neck and hands and the gauze pad taped to his left leg where a larger shard of plate glass had chewed into his flesh. He looked to his right, his skin still sticky-feeling from all the broken pop bottles and ruptured popcans that had sprayed all over him. He was glad it was winter—he wouldn't have wanted to make it home in mosquito season like that. The curtain parted that compartmentalized the emergency room unit he occupied from all of the rest and he recognized the face of the man who stepped through. He'd never seen him before, but the man was a police officer—Frost could read it in the eyes, the lines in the jowls and the set of the jaw. Intentionally, Frost thought, the guy shoved his coat back, putting his hands on his hips and showing what looked like a Cobra or Dick Special, nickel-plated, in a tension screw cross draw holster on his left side.

Frost leaned back on his elbows, raised his hands and cracked, "I didn't do it—whatever it is!"

"Bullshit—I checked you out, Frost. Sometime mercenary soldier, bodyguard with Diablo Protective Services—what the hell was that miserable bastard gunnin' for you for?" The man's voice was more southern Illinois than northern Indiana, Frost thought.

"You know my name—what's—"

The plainclothesman cut him off. "I'm Sergeant McGill—State Police homicide squad. The local guys saw you already, I understand."

"Yeah—couldn't tell them anymore than I can tell you," Frost started. "I was up early, antsy, decided to go out and get a gallon of milk from the store to go with my cereal. Maybe grab some more cigarettes, you know."

"Skip the shopping list, Frost," McGill snapped, walking over closer beside the table on which Frost lay, the curtain swatting closed behind him.

"Well, that's it, really. Had my track shoes on—over there," and Frost pointed to the chair in the corner of the enclosure and the sodden and stained track shoes in the small dark puddle next to it. "I walked inside the store, slipped on the floor—soles on the track shoes are pretty worn down and slick. That saved my life. That first shotgun blast came right through the door and the pellets hit the counter front just about the level of my belt. Would've cut me in half," Frost put in as an afterthought.

"You didn't see anybody at all when you came in?"

"No—just the car tracks and that's Jim Richards' car—he's the guy who manages the place."

"Did manage it," McGill said. "He told me he called his boss and quit rather than clean it up."

"Ahh, he's always quittin'," Frost smiled.

"Nothing else?" McGill persisted. "No sign you were being tailed or nothin'?"

"No," Frost said, thoughtfully. "I had a kind of crawly feeling on the back of my neck—you probably know the feeling," Frost said, pointing toward the gun McGill had on his belt. "And before the cops and the emergency people showed up, there were footprints in the lot across the snow leading to the back of the car from the hedge on the street side. Must've come up from there, I guess," Frost said. "Had to be his footprints but I think all the tire marks when the cops got there obliterated them."

"You got no idea why somebody'd want to knock you off, huh?"

"Well," Frost began, "you figure in my business I make enemies sometimes, but nothin' special." Frost's mind raced. Maybe the Mafia people he'd run up against in the thing with the Burmese drug warlords?* Frost hadn't gotten a good look at the man's face before he'd shot it off. A riot shotgun was sometimes an organized crime weapon, but somehow Frost didn't think it had to do with that. "No," he told McGill. "I really don't know. Get any kind of a make on the guy yet, maybe a name or something?"

"Yeah—as a matter of fact we did. I just got off the horn with Washington. We wired in prints off the guy—there wasn't enough left of his face for a photo. You play for keeps."

"There's another way?" Frost asked.

"Yeah, well—guy's a Cuban, jumped the immigration center right after he got in with all those others Castro let out on the boats a while back. Immigration people had him figured as not some ordinary refugee. Figured he was working for Castro and just infiltrated along with the real people looking for asylum. His prints turned up off a shotgun shell in a hit on an anti-Castro Cuban civic leader in Miami a month back. So, FBI guesses he's a hit man for Castro. So—you bein' a mercenary and all—you ever do anythin' Castro'd want you whacked for?"

Frost's salt and pepper stubbled cheeks creased into a grin. "Marina," Frost murmured.

"What?" McGill asked.

"Marina, I said," Frost said louder.

"What the hell this got to do with a boat dock?"

*SEE They Call Me The Mercenary #4, The Opium Hunter

"No—Marina—a girl's name. Marina Aguil-lara-Garcia. I was down down in Monte Azul, country down in Central America. Marina's father was anti-Communist and ran the country until the Castro terrorists made it so hot he had to leave. I was his bodyguard."

"Ain't that the guy that got gunned down in some kind of safe house near Mexico City?" McGill asked, pulling over a green plastic chair with his foot and turning the back around and straddling it.

"Yeah," Frost said, his voice low, the smile/frown lines downturned. "He's the one."

"Hell of a bodyguard you are," McGill cracked.

Frost pushed down the sheet covering his abdomen and drew his left hand across the row of scars there. "I did my best," he told McGill.

"Chopper?" McGill asked.

"Yeah—six rounds of 9mm—didn't need a colostomy, though," Frost answered.

"Revenge then?" McGill suggested.

"Could be that," Frost lied. He didn't think it was that, but he didn't feel like telling McGill his real suspicions.

"Could be that—well, hell, that's wonderful, Frost. I'll put that on my report, 'Could be revenge, victim says.' Then again," McGill snapped, "could be he just had nothin' else to do and said to himself I'm gonna smoke me a one-eyed man and you were the first one he bumped into. Bullshit. That guy had you staked out—you know it and I know it. Now, why?"

19

Shrugging, Frost began, "Well—Marina Aguillara-Garcia wants me to help her out and do some bodyguard work for her—maybe the Castro people got onto it and decided to stop me—I don't know."

Frost looked away from McGill then as a uniformed state patrol officer walked in through the curtains. Frost followed the man with his eye as the trooper walked over to McGill, leaned down and whispered something Frost couldn't catch. McGill nodded and as the trooper left, McGill looked up, saying, "Well—looks like there's a guy from State Department outside—wants to talk to you. Looks like too that according to them this is a clearcut case of international terrorism and you were just the luckless victim."

"Sorry," Frost shrugged, smiling.

"Yeah—like hell you are," and McGill stood up, looked over the corner to where Frost's clothes were, then grunted, "Man—you must be some kind of slob. I seen winos with better threads than that," and then McGill started toward the curtains.

Frost shouted after him, "When I got 'em at the store the salesman told me he'd sold something just like them to a fat state cop, so you got me!"

McGill stopped, his body tensing under his coat, then started toward the curtains again, not turning around as he ripped them aside and passed out of Frost's sight.

The curtains hadn't stopped swaying as they

opened again and a man with an expensive-looking leather attacheé case in his right hand walked in. He was tall, thin, with dark close-cropped hair and a high forehead. There was a spotless trenchcoat over the left grey-suited arm. The man stopped just inside the curtains, looked at Frost, looked around the room, then his gaze stopped. Frost followed the man's eyes—he was looking at the stained and sodden, blood-spattered clothes on the chair.

"Look," Frost snapped. "If you'd been covered with broken glass and bleeding and rolling around on a muddy floor when a bunch of pop bottles and cans blew up, you'd look like that, too—so no cracks."

"That's okay," the man said, smiling. "I can tell by that defensive tone that the last time you bumped heads with the State Department was under a previous administration, right?"

Frost thought for a moment. "More or less."

"Well—relax. We look at things a little differently in some areas. I'm not here to chew you out, threaten you or anything else. Besides, I don't think you threaten too well." The man reached into his briefcase and with two fingers extracted a plastic bag, Frost's sticky Metalifed High Power inside it. He walked the rest of the distance to where Frost lay and handed him the gun.

Frost looked at the plastic evidence bag, shook his head at the sight of the gun and laughed.

"My name's Beaton—Mike Beaton, Captain Frost—you must've been in one hell of a good

21

fight," and Beaton laughed.

Frost laughed too, setting the bag on the instrument table beside him, saying, "Yeah—I gotta admit it was different. God help the guy who owns the store though."

"Well—we decided to do a little something there, too," Beaton smiled. "Put in a kind word with his insurance company—he'll be out a hundred bucks deductible. But now what about you and that Castro hitman?"

"What about me—and the hit man?" Frost echoed.

"Well—we understand at State that Senorita Aguillara-Garcia is interested in hiring you as a, uhh—bodyguard? Right?"

Frost smiled, shrugging his shoulders. He was cold with just the sheet covering him. "She mentioned it several times—by telephone. I haven't given her any word yet—why?"

"Well, according to intelligence sources in Cuba, Castro is anticipating Senorita Aguillara-Garcia starting an invasion of Monte Azul within the next several weeks. Seems she has a mercenary army, plus the remnants of General Commacho's old army that still fight from the hills. Seems like all she's looking for is someone to lead the invasion and that has Castro and his puppet in Monte Azul—what's the guy's name?"

"Ernesto Ramon," Frost interjected.

"Yeah—looks like this Ramon character doesn't have much popular support down there. That, I think, is why Mr. Castro elected to have Raphael Ortiz try and kill you."

"Ortiz? That the guy's name?" Frost asked.

"Yeah—at least that's the name we've got on him. Doesn't matter if it's real or otherwise anymore, does it?"

"What do you want?" Frost asked bluntly. He was tired, cold and hungry and he needed a cigarette.

"Here—your file says you smoke these—take 'em," and Beaton handed Frost a fresh package of Camels and a book of matches.

"You read minds too?" Frost asked, his thumbnail already starting to rip at the cellophane. He opened the deck and pulled one of the cigarettes from it, reversed it and lit the end with the brand name.

"You've been on the run a lot, right?" Beaton smiled. "Old routine—smoke the brand name so nobody can tell you've been some-where—nowadays, though, the lab boys can analyze the tobacco for—"

Frost cut him off, "State Department or the Company, Mr. Beaton?"

Beaton smiled again, saying, "Maybe a little of both, Captain Frost. I understand when you were in Special Forces back in Viet Nam you wore two hats sometimes too."

Frost shrugged. He'd learned not to talk with strangers—and not from his mother. "What do you want?"

"Well," Beaton said, turning around a moment and setting his coat and attaché case on the chair McGill had used moments earlier, "all I want," and he turned and stared directly at

23

Frost, "is to know whether or not you plan to take that bodyguard job for Miss Aguillara-Garcia. Do you?"

"Why?"

"Well," Beaton said, smiling again, stretching his hands out palms up in an expansive gesture, "if you were to assume a military title you would run the risk of losing your citizenship. But, on the other hand, if all you did was bodyguard the young lady and understanding it would be a warlike situation you'd be involved with, well, we certainly would understand your peripheral involvement in the military activities going on around you—pursuant of course to your protective activities."

"Do you understand what you just said?" Frost asked sincerely. "I don't—you're saying go ahead and take the job with Marina, go help topple Ernesto Ramon, give Castro a good jab in the rear end?"

"Well—not in so many words, of course, but if you, ahh—"

"Why?" Frost asked, dragging deeply on the Camel and lighting a second one with the half-inch or so butt of the first one.

Beaton handed Frost a stainless steel bedpan to use as an ashtray and Frost nodded. "Well—we view Senorita Aguillara-Garcia as a friend of U.S. interests, a champion of democracy as it were—as was her father."

"He was a military dictator, right wing—he had his people's best interests at heart."

"Senorita Aguillara-Garcia spent some time in

24

the U.S., I understand she is interested in establishing a democratic—you'll pardon the expression—form of government and that the internal situation is ripe for a change. We only wish to make certain the lady is well-protected while she's doing this."

Frost stared up at the acoustical tile ceiling, watched the grey smoke from his cigarette drift upward. He thought about Bess—he still had to call her, he'd explain to her why. Marina had offered him one hundred thousand dollars, more money than he'd ever had. It could mean a future— He stopped thinking about it.

He closed his eye a minute, then opened it and focused hard on Beaton's professional smile. "All right," Frost said. "Why not?" There were a lot of reasons why not—Frost and Marina had been lovers and he'd left her, General Commacho's people would still want him dead for causing the train wreck that had killed Commacho in order to save Marina's father. And if the Castro people had tried to kill him before he'd made up his mind, he thought, now it would be a lead pipe cinch they'd go after him. He stubbed out the butt of the cigarette in the stainless steel bed pan. Inside in small letters were, "Made in U.S.A." He smiled—so was he.

Chapter Three

Frost loosened the black silk crocheted tie at
his neck, sweltering in the eighty-five degree
heat. He locked the door of the rented Ford and
crossed the broad palm-lined boulevard to the
comparatively ancient looking structure on the
other side—the Convent of Our Lady of Sor-
rows. He stopped on the opposite curb,
sunglasses on and his right eye still squinted
against the brightness. Northern Indiana had
been cold, then Chicago had been cold where
he'd taken the plane, and the blue blazer and
grey slacks he wore seemed now stiflingly warm.
He squinted down at his shiny black sixty-five
dollar shoes, then walked toward the double
wooden doors in the adobe looking wall, noting

26

the barbed wire strung for eighteen inches over the wall. People broke in anywhere these days, Frost mused.

He found a knocker on the doors and worked it, disappointed with the hollow sound against the soft wood. He pressed this thumbnail against the wood and it gave. There was a polished plaque on the stone pillar abutting the door on the right side, green around the edges and white where some of the polish hadn't been removed. In Spanish and in English it read "Erected 1887 Through The Loving Gifts of The People of Southern California for The Greater Glory of God and The Virgin Mother of Jesus."

Frost knocked again, then a small panel opened in the left hand door and Frost thought he could make out a woman's face behind it. "Yes?"

"Sister? My name is Hank Frost—I was told to say," and Frost gulped at the sticky sounding code phrase. "The bud of the rose is the promise of the spring."

The panel in the door closed and then the door itself opened. Frost stepped through. He stopped just inside the double doors and stared—a massive fountain dominated a verdant garden, fruit trees and flowers growing in neat harmony surrounding a flagstoned courtyard, the fountain at the center of it. He turned around, looking into the face of the short, slightly fat white-habited nun. "Did I pass, Sister?"

"The Senorita will join you in a moment, Captain—men are not permitted beyond the courtyard."

"I quite understand," Frost said, trying to sound pleasant rather than tired. At least it seemed cooler in the courtyard.

The Sister, one of the few Frost had seen in the United States in recent years who still wore the long habit, seemed to float across the courtyard as she left him. Frost shook his head, smiling, then sat on the stone bench beside the fountain trying to convince himself he felt cool. He had called Marina Aguillara-Garcia's people, she had called him back and they had settled on a price and a meeting place. She would pay one hundred thousand dollars. That was more money, Frost realized, than he had ever earned in his life. And mentally, he was already trying to determine what he would do with it. And again, he thought of Bess. It would now be the time to put up or shut up—he had always told Bess that when he got money, then . . . He had called her in London, spoken with her, encouraged her about the operation, told her about the job he was planning to do, at least as much as he'd felt safe in talking about over a trans-Atlantic phone line.

"What kind of a job is it, Frost?" Bess had said, her voice low, tense sounding.

"Well," he'd begun. "Kind of bodyguard thing, military situation—I know the people, worked for them before. It's a hundred thousand bucks, kid," he'd told her.

"Then what, Frost?"

"What do you mean? I mean, that's what we wanted—some serious, real money—a hundred grand, kid—"

"What's the good of it?" she'd interrupted, her voice tired sounding, "When you're dead, Frost—you can't spend it."

She'd been depressed about the operation to correct the last of the damage the bullet had done on her hip, depressed about not working for some time and bored, depressed about a lot of things, he'd thought. Frost stared down into his hands, saw himself balling his fists. He'd wanted to be with her for the operation, but instead . . .

"Hank—you came."

Frost looked up to the sound of the voice, then stood. "Marina," he said softly.

"If my father were still alive," the dark-haired, dark-eyed woman began, "he would have wanted you to do this, to come, to—"

"I'm here," Frost told her.

"Let us walk, Hank," she said, coming over to him, putting her left arm through his right and starting through the courtyard garden. "It will be a hard fight, but now that you will lead us I think we will win, retake Monte Azul."

"I can't carry a military title—technically I'll be your bodyguard."

"I know that—but titles do not matter, dear Hank. I didn't realize," she said, stopping and looking up at him, "how much I had missed you until I spoke with you by telephone that first time again. How have things been going for you?"

"The same," Frost shrugged, the salt and pepper stubbled smile-frown lines creasing into a grin, "the same. And how about you? Well, I assume, since you've been able to mount the

29

army and all.''

''It is not easy, Hank—I am a figurehead, a rallying point. I am expected to do this. Until I do, I can have no life of my own.''

''Do you think it will be any better afterward?'' Frost asked her.

''What do you mean?'' she asked, leaning her head against his right shoulder.

Frost ducked a low-hanging palm frond, saying, ''If you win, I mean. You'll have not only the entire nation of Monte Azul looking to you, but it would be the first major defeat for Fidel in Latin America—he won't take it kindly. Other nations will be looking to you—you know,'' Frost said.

''No life of my own?'' She stopped, Frost stopped and she turned to face him.

Frost looked down at her, felt her arms around his waist, her hands pressing up against his back. ''This moment is my own, Hank,'' she whispered.

Frost bent over her, his arms folding around her, her head cocking back—he remembered that first time he'd kissed her, in the place that had been her father's Presidential Palace, their faces and bodies streaming wet from the downpouring rain. Frost had been pushing into getting drunk that night. He wasn't now and he crushed her mouth under his. Her lips were moist, warm feeling and somehow sweet. He felt her hands moving up to encircle his neck, his hands holding her waist, his fingers splayed against her, their mouths searching each other. He closed his eye, remembering the rain, the wind from that balcony that first time, the chain lightning across the small lake near that palace—the surprise they'd felt that first time. As Frost kissed her in the convent garden, this time surprise, he thought, was replaced by desire . . .

Chapter Four

Two of Marina's bodyguards sat at a table across the room, two more waited in a car parked at the curb on the opposite street and two lounged near the front door of the restaurant. Frost had wanted to talk, they both liked Chinese food and so they had found a place Frost had visited one time before in the part of Los Angeles known as Hollywood. Frost hadn't remembered the name of the place and it had taken more than a half-hour of winding through the humid night streets in the three car caravan to find it. In the times Frost had been in Los Angeles, he had always felt the criticism of L.A. freeways and traffic in general was largely unfounded—he had worse times getting around in Atlanta and several other American cities. Manhattan was a disaster area during the rush hour.

Eight o'clock, muggy, a cool breeze blowing from somewhere intermittently, they found the restaurant, intentionally stepping on the brass looking stars in the sidewalk, Frost cracking he hadn't liked that actror or actess anyway, then gone inside and found a table. Small talk filled their conversation as they waited for the food—egg rolls, extra rice, sweet & sour shrimp. As the waiter brought the tea, Marina pouring, Frost asked, "So tell me about Ramon—what's he like?"

"Well, I'm sure you've read the papers, the newsmagazines—he's forty or so, handsome almost to the point where he looks effeminate. He is Castro's golden boy in a way. You know, he looks like a revolutionary leader, like something out of a romance novel."

"I don't read them," Frost smiled, lighting a Camel in the blue-yellow flame of his battered Zippo.

"Well," she laughed, "neither do I much—but that's what I hear. Anyway, Ernesto Ramon's real name is Francisco Peretta. He's not really from Monte Azul at all—the real Ramon was, and a good old family despite their left wing politics. I don't know what happened to the real Ramon, but Peretta is a Cuban, studied in Moscow, he was trained for the job he has. He's the ultimate puppet dictator—he doesn't just take orders—he's directly under Castro. And he is a butcher, too—this I know."

33

"What do you mean?"

"Well," she said, staring down at the small handle-less teacup, "after you kidnapped my father, and thee was the train chase out of Monte Azul into Mexico. The wreck, the one that killed General Commacho, it divided the anti-Communist forces in Monte Azul terribly. Commacho's nephew, Adolpho—he took the command and was running his own independent campaign against Ramon and his Government. But then Ramon started a purge. Newspaper editors, reporters, radio and television people, teachers—anyone who would tell the truth about Castro, Communism and Ramon—all killed or arrested and never heard from again. Finally, after many months, Adolpho communicated with me—he was willing to help and he and I could settle our differences after defeating Ramon."

"What differences?" Frost asked, stubbing out the cigarette, sipping at his tea.

"You—he holds me responsible for what happened, sees you as the murderer of his uncle. All this, more—imagined things, things he only knows the half truth of—it is an uneasy alliance, Hank. But I trust him until the battle is won. We both want to be rid of Ramon, to begin Monte Azul again. This time—I think my father was wrong—this time there will be a democracy. I will not be a self-proclaimed Presidenta, no?"

"You may have to be," Frost warned, stopping and waiting to resume talking until the waiter finished setting out the rice and shrimp and egg rolls. Frost tried one of the egg rolls, putting mustard sauce and sweet & sour sauce on it. He half whistled, "Whoo—these are hot—watch it!"

"There are two armies, as I told you," Marina continued. "Adolpho's Army working inside the country and the assault force you will lead—these are mercenaries, like yourself—" and she stopped and laughed. "Well, not quite like yourself. I have never met anyone quite like you. I have French, German, Canadian, anti-Castro Cubanos—some British, some American. They all wait for you to lead them."

"Why me?" Frost asked, softly.

"My father wanted that before his assassination by the Castro men at the house that night. You know that. There is no other man to lead my army but you—I trust you."

"It wasn't always that way, was it?" Frost smiled.

"Your motives and reasoning have been sometimes hard to understand," she said. "But I know you, I trust you—that is why I needed you."

"What did you tell them about me?" Frost asked her, trying the egg roll again, finding it still too hot and dishing rice and shrimp onto his plate.

"I told them you are sexy," she smiled, looking at Frost across the table, her feet rubbing against his under the table.

"Oh—that's terrific," Frost laughed.

"I told them what I knew—Special Forces in

Viet Nam, you tried civilian life for a while, then became a mercenary in Rhodesia at first, then throughout Africa, Latin America . . . And I told them never to bother you at night while you were sleeping with me.''

Frost looked at her across the table. "Are you propositioning me?"

"Si—yes, I am. Do you accept?"

Frost fell silent for a moment, then shrugged and said, "Only if you'll be gentle—" and they both laughed.

As dinner progressed, they discussed the composition of the Army she had waiting, the weapons available. It sounded too well-organized, Frost thought. And he wasn't as optimistic as she was, he knew—optimism to a degree was fine, but if it led to overconfidence it could destroy you. They passed on the vanilla ice cream and the fortune cookies—Frost distrusted fortune telling of any kind. It gave him the creeps, he knew. After settling on almond cookies, finishing the now tepid tasting tea, they made to leave the restaurant. "I hope those two enjoyed themselves," Frost told Marina, pointing at her two bodyguards across the room.

"I don't think so," she confided. "I don't think they like Chinese food," the girl laughed.

Frost stood, walked over to the other side of the table and helped Marina from the couch-type seat. She wore a dark blue, floral print sundress that bared most of her shoulders and back, sandals and a long strapped shoulder bag, her hair longer than he remembered it. She wore no jewelry other than a thin gold chain around her neck, and a gold ladies' Rolex on her left wrist. His hand at her elbow, glancing over his right shoulder for the two bodyguards, they started toward the door of the restaurant and out into the street, picking up the two bodyguards by the doorway. She said something to the four guards in Spanish, something too fast for Frost to catch. Shouldering her purse, she took Frost's left arm with both of hers and whispered, "I told them we would walk for a while and not to follow too closely."

Frost looked down at her. "I told you about that attempt on my life back in Indiana," he remarked. "You're asking for trouble."

"I'm not afraid with you."

"Ohh—I'm with me all the time. How come I'm afraid sometimes?"

She laughed, hugging his arm closer to her. The breeze from earlier had turned into a moderately strong wind, blowing toward them along the street as they walked now. Frost brushed his dark hair back from his forehead, turning and looking at the girl. The wind had caught her hair as well, making it dance almost from the nape of her neck, the mid-calf length skirt of the sundress pressed by the rush of air against her legs and outlining them under it. "Are you happy to be back with me?" she asked softly.

"Yes," he said honestly. "I am in a way, but . . ." and he let the sentence hang.

"You worry over the thing we do?"

He smiled, half at her, half at the occasional awkwardness of her English. "Yes," he told her. "In part that—yes."

"Was I too bold—you want to sleep with me, no?"

"I want to sleep with you again, yes," he answered, staring down the street, somehow uneasy. He glanced behind him, saw the bodyguards strolling perhaps a half-block back.

Frost stopped at the corner curb, stared at the traffic light—it was red. He stood there, waiting—but not for the light, he thought. He felt something. He looked down at Marina. "We can walk later—I've got a feeling. I don't know what, but—" He stopped in mid-sentence, hearing the rumbling of the car engine and the screech of tires and the whine of a power steering belt wrenched too hard all at once. Frost's right hand flashed under the left side of his blue blazer to the butt of the Metalifed Browning High Power there, his hand ripping the gun from the leather, his thumb jerking back on the hammer. With his left arm, he was already half sheltering, half moving Marina, back and away from the curb toward the side of the stone office building behind them. He could see the car now, windows open, cutting across into the oncoming traffic lanes of the broad street. "Fool!" Frost rasped. They should have come from the other side, Frost thought—he would have—then there could have been a gun from both the front and back seat, but with the driver's side being the business end, there was only one firing position.

Frost pushed the girl beside him down to the sidewalk, the High Power coming up in his fist, hearing himself shout to the bodyguards running up behind him, "Vaminos!" The car, a dark green four-door several years old, was wheeling closer to the curb, and in the darkness a split second before he heard the sound of gunfire from the rear, driver's side window, he could see the intermittent bright yellow muzzle flashes—a submachine gun.

Frost started firing the Browning, two shot bursts toward the subgunner, then alternating toward the driver's seat. He pushed Marina further back, falling on top of her as he kept firing, the submachinegun from the automobile back seat chipping a ribbon of pockmarks into the sidewalk and building front beside him, tearing into the mailbox, shattering a small display window. Frost raised his head, firing again, in the darkness of the front seat unable to see the driver behind the wheel but firing for him anyway, his shots walking onto the target, then Frost's trigger finger pumping the Browning as fast as he could, fighting the recoil to hold the gun on line as he sprayed into the driver's seat. The Browning's slide locked back, the magazine empty, Frost already buttoning out the magazine onto the pavement with his right thumb and snatching at one of the spares on the off-gun side of the shoulder rig. The car was coming up over the curb, out of control. As Frost rammed the fresh magazine home, he grabbed for Marina.

She screamed as Frost half dragged her by her

39

hair and the straps of her dress back away from the side of the building and the crashing automobile now jumping the curb, crushing the blue mailbox and ripping it from its anchoring on the sidewalk, the green auto half climbing the utility pole, the arc light suspended from it trembling and falling into the street with an explosion of glass.

Frost hauled Marina to her feet, edging back from the wreck, the subgunner in the rear seat half falling from the car, his gun blazing, Frost finally thumbing down the slide stop on the High Power. The slide rammed forward, stripping the first round from the magazine and chambering it, Frost's trigger finger working once, twice, then twice more, the subgunner doubling over onto his knees, the gun tumbling from his blood-streaming fists.

Frost pushed Marina behind him, edged forward a few steps and snatched up the magazine he'd dumped from the Browning a moment earlier, pocketing it, his eye never leaving the automobile. There was no movement from the green car. He started to sigh, to let his breath go and relieve the tension the minute, perhaps ninety seconds of the attack had built up in him. He started to, but stopped. The four bodyguards were nearly at the corner now, the car with the remaining two of Marina's guards had U-turned in the street and was racing down the block. But there was another sound—not the hammering of feet on pavement, or the revving of the eight-cylinder engine on the old Lincoln Continental coming toward them. It was a whirring sound. Frost had started to lower the hammer on the Browning. He jacked it all the way back now, the sound growing louder.

"Naw . . ." he muttered. They did it in movies, on television—not in real life. Then Frost shouted, "Marina—get down! Helicopter!"

Frost pushed the girl back into the nearest building front alcove, the chopper sweeping down over the broad four lane street from the windy darkness above, a machinegun already roaring in a continuous drone, the steel jacketed slugs hammering into the pavement, part of the burst eating into the gas tank of the green four door half climbing the utility pole, the black pockmarks along the left rear fender half-sawing it away from the car. Frost pushed Marina to the alcove floor, throwing himself over her, the gasoline in the tank exploding, the fireball of orange belching upward as Frost glanced skyward, then tucking his head down as the windows in the store front blew out on them. Pushing himself to his feet, Frost raised the Browning to fire against the helicopter, but the up-belching of flame from the automobile gas tank had already caught the bubble domed machine, a corona of fire around it for an instant. Frost pushed Marina down under him again, covering his own head with his hands and arms as the helicopter stopped in mid-air, perhaps thirty feet above the street, the roar deafening as it exploded. As the noise died, Frost

41

looked up, burning pieces of debris falling around him, some of it caught up on the wind, the heat from the fireball intense.

Frost hauled Marina to her feet, throwing his arms around her bare shoulders to shield her from the moment of searing flame. There was another explosion and Frost turned away, pulling the girl's head against his chest.

As the heat and sound died, Frost edged through the broken glass and burning bits of debris, out of the alcove. He glanced down the street. One of the four security men was dead—even from the distance the bloody row of red cutting a diagonal swath from right hip to left shoulder was unmistakable. The other three huddled around him. The windshield of the Lincoln was half clouded over with black from the fireball, the car stopped at an odd angle in the middle of the street, but now starting to move toward them.

Frost, still holding Marina tight beside him, glanced back into the intersection. The chunks of deformed steel and aluminum and plastic still burned and covered the center of the street and the sidewalk—there was a power line down, sparks flyng from it every second or so. The store fronts on all four corners had blown out windows, at least three different alarms discernible over the crackle of flames and the wind, the flames still giving an orange glow on the night as Frost looked down at Marina's face.

"Hank?" Her voice was like a whisper, or perhaps more like a little girl's voice.

"It's all right, kid," Frost rasped. The moral and legally correct thing would have been to wait for the cops, tell what had happened. Frost had no permit for the gun in Los Angeles, the helicopter, the car, the subguns Marina's guards had claimed from the Continental's trunk—it would have all taken so long the Cuban Communists would get time to set up another try.

Frost glanced back toward Marina's chief guard, Manuel. He waved for the car to pull up, rasping in Spanish, "Este camino esta cerrado—vamanos—salgase de aqui! Vamanos!" Frost smiled, starting the girl weakly toward the back seat of the Lincoln—he thought it was funny how his Spanish was coming back to him—but the grammar was just as bad as it had ever been.

Manuel was also the wheelman, and he bootlegged in the street with the second car with the three still living of the four bodyguards who had been on the street and the body of the dead one right behind them. Frost pushed the button for the automatic window—he needed to breathe and the wind was cool.

Chapter Five

Frost stood up in the prow of the small outboard and stared ahead of him toward the three freighters looming up from the horizon. He felt almost ridiculous, the titleless general coming to take command of his Army—which happened at the moment to be a Navy. He turned to Marina, sitting a yard or so behind him. "Just like Washington crossing the Delaware, huh?"

She returned his smile with a blank stare and he shrugged his shoulders. After the battle outside the Chinese restaurant, they had returned to the beachhouse Marina had been using under an assumed identity, she had showered and changed, then they had sat up through the rest of the night. Finally, an hour before dawn, Frost had fished some things out of his luggage, taken a shower, shaved, dressed and had breakfast. With no sleep for pushing thirty-six hours, his camouflage fatigues still showing creases and his gear stowed in the small craft, Frost was about to assume command. He laughed at the thought. "General Frost," he muttered. His fatigue blouse showed no rank emblem, and he wasn't about to change that. He sat down, staring across the glassy calm of the water.

"Marina," Frost said.

"Si, Hank?"

"Ingles, por favor," Frost said. The man running the small boat spoke only Spanish.

"What is it, Hank?" she asked again.

"Just because I wear a beret like he did, sometimes, I'm no Montgomery. I'm no general at all, kid—my only way is to get in there and fight. And some of those people may have outranked me in the armies they came from. This isn't going to go too smoothly."

"Hank," she said, the only sounds other than her voice the lapping of the water that was the small boat's wake and the putt-putting of the outboard. "My father, myself—there are plenty of Generals in the world. There are not plenty of men who never give up—I remember you on the train, after they had tortured you, after the wreck when the Communists attacked. There are perhaps men who are stronger, shoot straighter, may be better strategists—you are—como se dice," she paused. "You are unique. I have seen you fight only because there was breath still in your body and an enemy to be killed. That is why you and no one else must be my General, darling.''

Frost shrugged, not knowing what to say. It was rare that someone complimented him.

"All right—but you've got too good an opinion of me. There's nothing noble about fighting—I'm just too dumb to fall down, kid—that's all.'' He saw her reaching her hand across to him and he took it. Her dark eyes almost seemed to glow in the early morning sunlight and there was a life and vitality in her face that hadn't been there a moment earlier. "All right—you got a general, Marina.''

The small boat moved in toward the center of the three freighters, the ships, rusty looking hulks, anchored offshore just outside territorial waters. Frost decided Marina had developed pull with the government—otherwise the Coast Guard would have been sitting all over the ships, waiting for them to move. Docking beside the middle ship, Marina climbed the steps leading to the deck, Frost behind her, the boatman going back for Marina's things on the larger craft they had left a mile or so behind.

As Frost reached the main deck, he stopped, half crouched from the ladder, standing beside the railing. Aboard the ship on the main deck were several hundred men—he wasn't sure how many. All wore various types of fatigues, some of the faces were white, some black, a few even Oriental. Various sidearms and knives hung from pistol belts or shoulder holsters, the

46

headgear ranging from berets to slouch hats like Frost himself wore.

A booming, British sounding voice, shouted, "Ten-hut!" The mercenary force came to attention almost as one man, Frost still staring. The man belonging to the British voice strode forward, approached Frost and threw up his right hand in a classic, almost stagey looking British palm forward salute. "Sir!"

Frost looked at the British soldier, then looked at Marina—who positively beamed.

Shrugging his shoulders, Frost turned back to the Briton and returned the salute. There was no rank that Frost could see. As the Britisher lowered his salute, Frost asked, "Who's in charge here—yourself?"

"Yes, sir!"

"Stand easy, huh," Frost implored.

The Britisher echoed Frost's request to the rest of the men, then himself stood down.

Frost stood there, not knowing what to say—he wasn't recently used to military protocol. They finally, Marina said, "I promised the men you'd address them—Hank?"

Frost looked at her and smiled, "Well, I would address them, but I'm terrible at remembering zip codes—anyway, I don't have any stamps."

She didn't laugh and Frost shrugged again, groaning, "All right." From the corner of his eye he spotted a ladder leading up to a smaller deck near the prow of the ship and Frost walked toward it, mounted it halfway and began to speak. "My name is Hank Frost," he said. From the rear there was a voice, shouting, "Louder."

Frost nodded and began again. "I'm Hank Frost—sometime Captain. I'm not a general, but for the sake of this operation I'm the man in charge militarily. I understand from Senorita Aguillara-Garcia that she's briefed you all on my background. As I get around and meet some of you I'm sure we'll find there are common outfits and things like that where maybe we've served in the past. Now, contrary perhaps to what you might think, this deal isn't going to be easy, nor is it going to be impossibly difficult. It's going to be tough, probably—definitely—some of you who are standing here today are going to wind up pushing up the Monte Azul version of daisies—some of you won't be that lucky. But the son-of-a-bitch running Monte Azul, Ernesto Ramon, is a damned Communist, works for old friendly Fidel. So we all have a stake in puttin' him out of business." Frost was tempted to stop, but saw an expectant look in the eyes of many of the men and decided then to talk a little more.

"I've worked in Monte Azul. I know the people a little—once it looks like we're putting Ernesto Ramon's tail between his legs, we should pick up support. One last thing—" and Frost lit a Camel in the blue yellow flame of the Zippo, cocking the camouflage crusher hat down low over his eyes as the sun loomed high against him.

"This is going to be a largely seat-of-the-pants operation—I'll get around to appointing a staff in a few days as soon as I know who for what. There's been an attempt on my life and last night

48

a good-sized shot to get the Senorita and myself. So we can't sit around here anymore than we have to. We've gotta move in as fast as possible. Now—in five minutes up on the deck behind me I want the following—the Britisher I spoke with," and Frost gestured toward the man, "any man who's held rank of Captain or above in any actual army or other military unit, the captain of this ship and the two others and Senorita Aguillara-Garcia." Then Frost shocked himself by saying, "Now—I don't know anybody's preferences or anything . . ." Maybe, he thought, it was because Marina had told him he was her General. "But why don't we all just hang loose a second and if anyone wants to, ahh—well, they can."

Some of the men bowed their heads, some fidgeted nervously. After a moment, Frost glanced down at the Britisher and said, "Why don't you dismiss the men?" Then Frost turned and started toward the upper deck. "This General business," he muttered under his breath . . .

There was a canvas tarp strung out over a part of the deck, half of it running from what Frost assumed might be the wheelhouse. The Britisher—once a Sergeant-Major with the Special Air Service—the captains of each of the three ships and about twenty other men, all at one time Captain or above, stood assembled around Frost and Marina, Frost chain smoking. Frost had learned so far that there were 984 men, including the crew members for the three ships, and they too could be counted on to fight. There was enough in the ships' stores that the tiny armada could survive without landfall for fourteen days without hard rationing, nearly twice that long with it. Sanitation facilities were decent if not attractive and there was no evidence of vermin. All told, conditions were better than Frost had imagined they might be. There were various weapons aboard beyond those the individual men of the company had brought with them—supplies of M-l6Als, .45 caliber grease guns, an assortment of Smith & Wesson .38 Special revolvers and Colt. 45 automatic pistols, Government and Commander Models. There were two dozen M-60 machineguns, at least that many 3.5-inch Rocket launchers—Bazookas—some LAWS rockets Frost didn't even inquire about as to origin and there were various assorted light machineguns and submachineguns in the inventory as well. Explosives supplies looked good—various types of plastic, some old fashioned dynamite, various types of grenades—no mines. Frost was mildly disturbed at the latter—in case they got stalled on the beachhead it would limit defensive capabilities. There was one relatively huge deck gun which Frost promised himself to investigate. He'd already made plans to supplement this if necessary and practice with a special force of "deck gunners" armed with M-79 Grenade Launchers—there was a ridiculously ample supply of HE (High Explosive) projectiles. The only item of small arms sadly lacking was sniper rifles—there were no provisions for these. Frost made the on-the-spot decison to recruit the best ten riflemen among the near thousand man force and give them the pick of the M-l6Als available and that this would have to do.

After the last of the accounting of supplies and equipment, Frost turned to Marina, cracking, "This isn't a big budget picture, is it?"

"What?" she asked.

"Never mind," Frost shook his head.

Turning to the ex-Sergeant Major, Frost asked, "Let's start with you—I didn't catch you name."

"Timmons, sir!" the big Britisher beamed.

"Timmons—fine. Okay, Mr. Timmons—let's for the time being at least have you serve as my chief of staff—whatever kind of title you want really, just be my number two, okay?"

"Very good, sir!"

Frost, his right eye squinted against the sun, his forehead dripping sweat, said, "Fine—then two things. First, get things co-ordinated with the Captains of these tubs and let's get underway if that's the right terminology. And secondly, cut out the formal crap, huh? Get me the charts showing our course once we're moving. I'll be downstairs or below or whatever checking the equipment."

Frost self-consciously returned Timmons' salute but smiled, noticing the man had at least stopped with the 'sirring' and looking as though he were advertising backbraces.

With Marina beside him, he started toward the

51

main deck, past some of the men still transferring to the other ships and toward the main hold which had been converted into a massive arms locker for all three ships. As they entered the hold, past the security and into the weapons storage area, Frost whispered conspiratorially to the girl, "Well, did I come off sounding more like U.S. Grant or maybe Patton?"

The girl laughed and squeezed his arm. "We have a special gun for you down here—come and see it. I remembered you liked it from before."

Frost followed her toward the boxes of rifles and the half filled racks behind them—most of the weapons hadn't even been unpacked. The girl stopped at the end of the nearest of the racks. Frost reached into the rack and smiled. It was what he called a CAR-16, though such a weapon didn't really exist. Externally, it was identical to the civilian semi-automatic CAR-15 which he used frequently. But, the gun was specially modified with the necessary automatic fire components to work semi- or full-auto, like the military M-16A1. Frost liked the collapsible stock feature, but it was not to be found in the military configuration since the obsolescence of the XM177 series rifles. In a strict military situation, Frost liked selective fire weapons, but for security work, unlike many others in the field, he preferred semi-automatic firearms, considering a well-placed two-round semi-automatic burst with a handgun or rifle as effective or more so than a spray from a full auto weapon.

Frost took the weapon from the rack, tweaked

the ears on the bolt and checked the chamber. Letting the bolt forward, he snapped the trigger on the empty chamber and began hunting thirty-round magazines and ammunition. As he loaded six spare magazines for the modified Colt rifle, he began talking. "Why me—I've gotta ask again? Even this—you were waiting for me, weren't you?"

"Si—but to answer the suspicion in your mind," she said, rubbing the palms of her hands against the sides of her blue jeans. "I did not set you up with that killer back in Indiana."

"Well," Frost admitted, looking around to make certain he wasn't near any explosives, "that did cross my mind—but only for a moment." He lit a cigarette with the Zippo as he finished one of the magazines, slipping the last round under the feed lips and back above the pressure of the other twenty-nine rounds over the follower. He set the scratched Parkerized magazine down and began loading another. He recognized the ammunition—a common surplus variety he'd used before with acceptable results. "Here—once I find someone to be the armourer we'll get this one fixed," and Frost handed the girl one of the magazines, grabbing up a fresh one for himself. "The feed lips are bent out of shape."

"You are an expert, no—with guns?" the girl smiled.

"Well," Frost sighed. "Certain guns, maybe. Good friend of mine, writes paperback novels, magazine articles, now he's pretty much of an expert with handguns, okay with assault rifles, riot shotguns, but I don't think he'd know a trap stock from a skeet stock with a sporting shotgun. Most experts, if they're really experts, are limited to a certain field." Frost shrugged again and went back to loading the last magazine.

Frost ferreted around the makeshift armory and found a canvas rucksack, then loaded the magazines for the "CAR-16" into it, along with the spare magazine for the Interdynamics KG-9 he pulled from the waistband of his fatigue trousers. The KG-9 he pulled from his belt where he'd shoved it before boarding the freighter and stuffed it in the bag as well. "Feel lighter already," he smiled, picking up the sack and starting with the girl toward the ladder or companionway—he wasn't certain of the term—leading out of the hold and to the main deck. They were halfway up, the CAR-16 slung diagonally across his back, muzzle down, thirty-round magazine in place, when there was a rumbling sound, then the entire vessel shook and the girl, on the ladder like stairs above him, stumbled, starting to fall back. Frost reached forward, grabbing her roughly at the waist, the girl leaning against the railing, running a hand through her hair.

"What was that!" she half-screamed.

"You tell me, kid—it's your boat," Frost rasped, pushing past her and taking the steps two at a time. "Come on," he shouted over his shoulder to her.

Frost hit the main deck, stopping half in the

well of the stairway leading out of the hold, black smoke—chokingly thick—starting to pour across the main deck, belching from a ragged hole in what Frost guessed they called the after-deck. He saw Timmons, the bulldog-like Sergeant Major, a fire axe in his hands but not running toward the fire, running instead after a blonde-haired man charging across the main deck.

Frost jumped from the stairwell and hurtled himself toward the man, knocking him to the deck, rolling over on top of him, then crossing the man's jaw with his right fist in a short arc, the man's head lolling back.

Frost pushed himself to his feet, snatching at Timmons with the fire axe, the axe already back for a swing into a death blow, "Hold it! Damnit, that's an order, Timmons!"

"He's the bloody bastard what did—"

"Slow down," Frost snapped, letting go of the axe of the handle, Timmons swaying back from the man on the deck, Frost and Timmons both starting to cough.

"He put a plastic charge there—one of my lads saw him with it in the engine room, started chasing him. The bastard had a knife and cut Davey cruel with it, but Davey shouted and some of us came running up. He just threw the bloody charge and killed one of the Japanese blokes and a German and nearly got me too. Bloody Castro-Commie," and Timmons raised the axe again, Frost reaching out, grabbing it and hurtling the axe into the deck, the bit biting into the

55

weathered boards, the handle quivering.

"Let's take care of the fire first, then we take care of him!" Frost grabbed one of the officers he recognized from the deck meeting moments earlier, shouting, "Watch him—and keep him alive," then Frost started running toward the source of the fire and smoke. Marina was already on deck and Frost tossed her the canvas bag and his rifle, shoving the latter into her arms as he ran past, then took the steps leading up to the afterdeck three at a time. The heat was scorching as Frost started toward the source of the smoke then fell back. Wheeling, he shouted to the Britisher behind him, "Timmons—get a fire brigade organized—and fast." Timmons started off into the throng of men on the after-deck, Frost grabbing the man nearest him, shouting, "Get some rope, get some buckets and start hauling water," then grabbing at some of the other men, "You, you, get the lead out—move it!"

Frost raced along the deck, spotting the Captain, grabbing the man, wheeling him around roughly on his heels, Frost's hands gripping his shoulders, "What's down there?"

"Ahh—sleeping quarters mostly—but nobody moved in really—most of the men came in so late last night they slept topside. Not much else—some rubber boats."

"Good—take ten men, get down there with some fire equipment and start after it—we'll be pouring in water from topside—hurry, man," Frost snapped, half-shocking the Captain into action.

Turning, Frost spotted Timmons already coming up to the afterdeck, a dozen men streaming behind him, hoses and axes in hand, the hose nozzle already dripping sea water.

Frost ran toward Timmons, half hauling the big man around, "Radio room—where?"

"Up by the wheel house, sir."

"Get on with it, " Frost rasped, shoving past the men still coming with more hose, fighting his way halfway down the row of steps, then flipping the railing and landing on the deck, coming up out of the crouch and breaking into a dead run. He reach the other side of the lower deck, then took the steps there three at a time, hauling himself up to the foredeck and racing across to the wheelhouse.

He stopped, catching himself against the wheelhouse door, half throwing himself inside.

There was a pale-faced young man, standing there looking through the open wheelhouse windows back toward the afterdeck. "Get on the radio," Frost rasped— "get those other two ships over here—I want both Captains now."

"Who the bloody hell are you?" the pale-faced man snapped.

"I'm the godddamned C.O.," Frost replied, edging forward.

"Sorry—ahh," and the man half fell into the chair behind the radio set and worked his hands over a series of switches and started calling, "Angel One to Angel Two and Three—come in, over!"

Frost grabbed the microphone from the

younger man, rasping into it, "This is Frost—I'm on the boat with the fire—you know. Get your collective rear ends over here on the double, start pumping water across into that fire—Angel Two," and Frost didn't know which ship was which, "come up on your nearest side, Angel Three do the same—pronto."

Frost dropped the microphone and ran back across the foredeck and down the steps leading to the main deck and across it again, then up to the afterdeck and the firefighting brigade. Buckets were moving at a fantastic pace, water spilling everywhere, hoses spraying down into the jagged hole in the deck, the smoke starting to subside slightly, Frost judged. Frost pushed himself to the front of the fireline, Timmons wrestling a hose, Frost shouting to him, over the din, "I've got the other two ships coming in—send two men down to get the Captain and his team to pull back. When that water comes it's going to be a lot. Keep the Captain standing by—you do it yourself. I'll take over here. Keep the Captain standing by near enough to the fire that we can shut off the water works when the fire's under control before we start listing too badly—take someone with you."

"Right you are sir," Timmons shouted, shoving the hose nozzle to Frost. Frost at last realizing how strong the Britisher was, the hose bucking in Frost's hands for a moment as he tried wrestling it into position.

The hose aimed properly, Frost braced himself to keep it that way, water belching out in irregular and powerful spurts, pumped Frost knew from the sea around them. From the corner of his right eye, Frost could already see the ship on the port side in position, water starting to pour over from the vessel, Frost, the men around him instantly sodden and almost knocked to the deck. On his knees to control the hose now and resisting the residual spray from the other ship, Frost aimed the firehose into the hole. In minutes, the second ship was on line, its hoses spraying, the afterdeck surface slick as glass, the spray from both hose lines making a rain like a tropical downpour.

The firefighting went on for a time Frost couldn't gauge, his hands and arms weary from wrestling the hose. Suddenly beside him, Frost heard Timmons, "Sir—Captain of Angel One says the fire is struck—he wants to begin pumping operations to clear the hold."

Frost nodded to the Britisher, shouting, "Alert the pump crew on our deck, then get to that radio man and have him signal the Angel Two and Angel Three to shut down and stand by in case the pumping operation goes badly or the fire starts up again."

"Right you are, sir!" and Timmons bounded off, Frost's neck muscles strained, his hands bone weary as he held onto the hose for what he knew were the last few minutes. The pressure slacked—he could feel it in his hands before he felt it in the hose. As it slacked more, the water dribbling by comparison to its earlier force, Frost dropped the hose to the deck and tried getting to his feet. His knees, his back—suddenly Frost felt the exhaustion of the battle with the fire.

On his feet, he half staggered toward the railing and made it down the stairs, leaning hard against the railing. He spotted Timmons, saw Marina, and he saw the blond-haired man, the arsonist, the saboteur. Walking, stiffly, slowly, Frost threw his crusher hat to the deck, loosed the sodden pistol belt at his waist and shoved it toward Timmons, Timmons' hands edging to the protruding butt of the High Power. Frost walked ahead, the Gerber knife coming from his waist and he tossed it down, stopping finally inches from the blond-haired man, their faces almost touching.

The man was fully conscious, a look in his eyes Frost didn't like. Frost snapped, "What do they call you?"

"Grunwald . . ."

"You work for Castro's people, for Ramon, who?"

"Go to hell," the blond man, Grunwald, snapped, half laughing.

"Let him go," Frost rasped to the two men holding Grunwald. The two men—one a black Frost recognized, the other a red-haired white man, stepped away. Grunwald stood, unmoving, the glare in his eyes still there but muted. "One more time—who hired you?"

"Go to . . ." the man started again.

Frost started to haul his right back, shoving his left forward as if to grab at the man's clothes.

Frost slammed his left knee upward, catching the man hard in the groin, the cold glare gone from the ice blue eyes now, replaced by pain and surprise. Frost's left hand clenched into a fist and jabbed into the center of Grunwald's face, catching Grunwald as he started doubling over from the groin shot, doubling the force of Frost's blow. Blood sprayed in Frost's face as he took a half step forward, his right fist hammering forward catching the blond-haired man on the left side of the head and driving him down.

Frost stepped back, Grunwald rolling on the deck, then starting to his feet. Frost made to lean down, to grab Grunwald and haul him up, and as Grunwald started to grab for Frost's fists, Frost lashed out with his left foot, the toe of his sodden black combat boot catching Grunwald at the tip of the chin and knocking the man up and flipping him back. Frost inched toward Grunwald. "Who—come on, asshole—who hired you!"

Grunwald started to his feet and Frost stepped in, his left fist hammering hard into the red and pink meat of the man's left cheekbone, knocking Grunwald back. Frost, his teeth clenched, rasped, "I don't believe in torture—" and Frost's right fist hammered outward like a piston as Frost wheeled on his left foot, changing his guard and throwing his body behind the punch, "but I don't believe in," and Frost's right hammered into Grunwald's mouth, Frost's knuckles splitting on the teeth, Grunwald's lower lip spouting bright red blood. "I don't believe,"

61

Frost began again, "in assassins, and butchers and damned saboteurs either—I'll keep this up all," and Frost made to come in with his left, feigned instead and threw his right in a short hook under Grunwald's chin, more blood spattering from the man's face. "I'll keep this up longer than you can," and Frost crossed Grunwald's outstretched chin with his left fist, hammering the man against the rail. "Come on, you son of a bitch—can't you fight without a goddamned chunk of plastic," Frost roared, his hands grabbing for Grunwald.

Grunwald's right knee came up, Frost seeing it, stepping away from most of the force of it. Frost's right lashed outward, across Grunwald's face, impacting against the left cheek and glancing off against the nose, Grunwald falling from Frost's grasp and over the rail, his body tumbling into the water below. Frost bent down, his fingers, still stiff starting to fumble at the laces of his combat boots. "Hell," he rasped, then stepped to the rail, stepped over it and stared down into the water and jumped.

Frost hit the water hard, ducking under the surface to break the dive, coming up and seeing Grunwald, grabbing for the man, losing him, "Come here!" Frost shouted.

As Frost swam after Grunwald, he stopped, treading water, Grunwald, facing him in the water now, a knife in his right hand, the blade slicing toward Frost, skimming over the water. Frost dove, his hands reaching out, catching at Grunwald's ankles, pulling the blond-haired man under the water. The knife was coming down, Frost could see it.

Frost let go, pushing himself back from Grunwald, the swing still coming, Frost throwing himself forward, grabbing at the knife arm. Frost's left hand caught Grunwald's right forearm, Frost's right hand hammering through the water into the elbow above the knife hand, the elbow snapping, Frost's knuckles aching and on fire.

Frost pushed his head above the water, wrestling Grunwald up by his broken arm, Frost's right hand slapping the man back handed across the face. "Who hired you?" Frost rasped.

Grunwald stared to mumble something, Frost hauled on the man again to keep him out of the water, then rasped again, "Who?!"

"Ramon—spy on you—sabotage you—I'll talk," the man stuttered.

Frost shoved the man away from him, treading water as he shouted, "Timmons—get a boat over the side to grab this man—then get the doctor or whatever we got to patch him up." Frost started swimming back toward the boat, the Angel One. He felt stupid, angry and his hands hurt and his knuckles were raw. He didn't like what he'd done—but he didn't like guys like Grunwald either.

Chapter Six

Frost sat on the deck by the wheelhouse, staring ahead of the bow of the battered freighter, Angel One. The name amused him, Angel One. He knew who the angel was—Marina, and there were various ways of interpreting the word. The three ships—Frost would have called them Nina, Pinta and Santa Maria—had gotten underway by early afternoon and now, night falling already on the portside, his left toward Baja California somewhere lost in a deep purple, the sun was setting to his right, the ocean there, unbroken seeming to him, gold flecked and orange as the sun seemed to sink and sizzle into it. There was a cool breeze and Frost had already determined he'd sleep on the foredeck. Ostensibly, he would be near the wheelhouse of the ship, near the radio room, on call for trouble—secretly, however, he thought below decks would be hot, the smoke smell would be there too and despite the total absence of any signs of vermin, Frost had no desire to find out first hand there were rats. They had patched up Grunwald and sent him by small boat back toward the yacht from which Marina and Frost had come that morning, the crew of the yacht to take Grunwald back to the coast and drop him off—Frost had no desire to execute the man. Once aboard, Grunwald had volunteered that Ramon had hired him to infiltrate the crew of one of the freighters but he had instead signed on as one of the mercenaries. After Grunwald had left, Frost had thought better of it almost wishing he'd kept the man a prisoner aboard. Hindsight's problems notwithstanding, Frost had decided, he had had Timmons organize a thorough bomb and incendiary device search of all three ships. Unless something ultra-sophisticated had been done to the weapons, etc., nothing had been found. That only tended to make Frost feel more nervous. Another reason, he decided, for not sleeping below decks.

Frost watched the orb of sun, huge there on the sea—he had spent little of his life on the water. Life—he had spent little of his life doing anything he'd particularly wanted, he reflected. Now, most of all, he wanted to be somewhere else—in London with Bess for the operation. But he needed the hundred thousand dollars, for both of them.

In Viet Nam he'd done about every dirty job they'd had—led a sniper team, led a team that had worked deep inside V.C. territory, deep inside the North—it had always been, "Get Frost—he can do it," and Frost had done it. The loss of the eye had changed it all but once more, Frost realized, remembering Marina's wanting him and no one else to lead her counter revolution, it was still get Frost.

His thoughts turned then to the battles ahead once they reached the objective of Monte Azul—if they reached it, he reminded himself. Ramon knew their timetable, or thought he did, and would try to cut them off somehow. Frost had already determined that the obvious, original plan would not be followed, there would be no more communication with the forces of Commacho's nephew until the attack was almost imminent.

"A hell of a time for strategy," Frost thought. He turned, hearing footsteps behind him—Marina. "What are you doing here?" the one-eyed man asked her.

"I came to talk—the men talk about you below. They say you are brave, a good commander."

"Good for the men," Frost rasped, lighting a cigarette, staring at the sunset. He felt the woman's arms around his neck, her hot breath against his cheek. "You tryin' to tell me something?" Frost smiled.

"What do we do, Hank—our next move is—"

"I don't know about your next move, " Frost

began, taking the girl in his arms and leaning over her. The orange from the sun caught on the skin of her hands and face, burned like a fire, he thought, in the dark centers of her eyes. He felt her hands in his hair at his neck, his own hands pressing against the work shirt she wore to feel the skin beneath it. Suddenly there was a roar, a single scream piercing the night over the steady throbbing of the ship's engines, Frost pushing himself up on his hands and then to his feet, his left hand snatching for the CAR-15 on the deck beside where he'd lain with the girl. "Holy God!" he shouted, staring away from the sunset and toward Angel Two. "Holy God!" There was another roar now, the girl standing beside him, throwing herself against him, her head going against his chest. Frost held the rifle in his left hand and still holding it, folded his left arm around the girl's shoulders. "Fool I am," Frost rasped, running for the wheelhouse from the half blind side where he'd been, the Angel One Captain, Pietro Torres, "Blackie", already stepping half out onto the deck. Running, Frost shouted, "Captain—get on that radio and get a situation report—pronto, mucho pronto!"

Frost stopped, beside the wheelhouse, hearing the rasping whispers and static over the radio inside, hearing the sounds of running feet on the deck of his own ship, listening, helpless for the moment, as another explosion rocked the guts of Angel Two—but still there was no fire visible.

Frost moved into the wheelhouse, snatching the microphone from the Captain, half-shouting

67

over the next roar, "What the hell is going on?"

"Explosions in the boiler room—fire everywhere aft of the main hold burning out of control!"

"Shit!" Frost snapped. "This thing work into the ship speaker system?"

"Si?"

"Hit the right button," Frost snapped, then punching the microphone push to talk switch, he began, "This is Frost—now hear this." He remembered that from a movie about the World War Two Navy. "Now hear this—Timmons, wherever you are get to the foredeck as quick as you can, organize a fire team on the way to assist the Captain of Angel Two. Next, I want one volunteer to man each of our lifeboats, and volunteers to get them over the side. Timmons—where's that fire crew?" and Frost killed the mike. "Patch me into Angel Three," Frost told the radio man.

"Aye, sir," the man returned. "Go ahead."

"Frost to Angel Three, come in."

"Angel Three reading you loud and clear, sir."

"Get over on the far side of Angel Two on the double—"

"On my way, Captain Frost—already under power."

"Roger that," Frost snapped. "Get a fire crew—the same number you did for us earlier, and get every life boat you can to the Angel Two on the double."

"Aye sir," the Captain of Angel Three returned.

"Frost out," and Frost handed the microphone back to the radio man, running from the radio room, spotting Timmons on the deck below and shouting to him, "Get your crew going now—pick some to co-ordinate the lifeboat effort," Frost added.

Frost turned back toward the wheelhouse, remembering he'd just assumed the Captain of Angel One—Blackie—would get underway to get closer to the stricken Angel Two, but as Frost started moving back toward the wheelhouse he could already feel the deck under him shifting as the Angel One came hard to port toward the center ship.

Frost walked, slowly because hurrying would avail him nothing, toward the railing off the port bow, watching the Angel Two, waiting for the fires to break through the main deck and become visible. He could blame Grunwald, he told himself, but the blame was more with himself. There should have been some way to have learned Grunwald wasn't the only Communist agent in the company. Should have been, he told himself. That was the best security, independent operatives who didn't know each other—that way there was no possibility they behaved suspiciously toward one another.

Frost turned to his right a second, feeling Marina beside him, looking down at her, "What will happen, Hank?"

Frost began to say, "I don't," but stopped himself. In the girl's eyes he saw something, in the way she had asked him what would happen, in the way she had wanted him and no one else. It was the thing with her father—the trust she'd had in General Aguillara-Garcia, the white haired rapier straight leader—she had transferred that trust to him. "It will be all right—somehow," Frost told her, the words meaningless to him, feeling the girl's head resting against him, Frost turned and watched Angel Two—flames had broken through the main deck now, high, hot, orange-yellow flames that licked and crackled in the sea's breeze, but somewhere in it Frost could hear the screams of the men the lifeboats weren't going to have to save . . .

Frost had joined Timmons and his fire crew and until they were weary, they had fought the blaze through the night, rescuing each man they could, rescuing all the supplies they could—they had lost forty-two men, some of their bodies recognizable, some not, some of the bodies never found before the Angel Two had begun listing so badly the decks were two-thirds awash and Timmons and Frost had boarded the last lifeboat, the two oarsmen sweating, working frantically to get clear of the dying ship before it started down and its undertow dragged the fragile lifeboat along with it. Marina had organized the galley crew to get coffee and sandwiches going and, working into the next dawn Frost, Timmons, Marina and two of Timmon's men, along with the Captain of Angel One, Blackie Torres, had inspected every inch of Angel One and Angel Three, opened every box, done everything short of opening every can and every grenade and rocket. But there were no explosives.

Smoke still hanging in a cloud over the two ships, the ships perhaps forty yards apart, the sea calm, Frost stood at six forty-five that morning on the foredeck of Angel One, using a loud hailer or bullhorn, addressing those still alive to hear him."We still have a traitor, maybe more than one aboard the two ships. Unless we all turn around and go home, we can count on him doing something else to sabotage our mission. There could be just one man, there could be more. We can't go around looking at everyone as though he were a bomber or saboteur—we'll never win that way, we'll never even survive. I'm meeting with all of the surviving people I met with yesterday—Captains and above. We'll be organizing into ten man teams—and those ten men will live together, work the same shifts, everything. No one goes anywhere alone on this ship except for myself or Senorita Aguillara-Garcia. Any man caught alone is automatically shot, by me."

Frost waited as the audible murmuring of dissent began to die down, then went on, "If we don't get this to work as a self-policing technique, then we may as well hang it up—if anybody has a better suggestion, pass it along to me through one of the men Captain or above or through Mr. Timmons. If it's a better idea, I'll love it. And one last thing," Frost said, his voice low and hoarse and whiskey-sounding from no sleep. "If there is another traitor aboard and we find you—if you are aboard and are hearing my voice and surrender now, I pledge no harm will come to you, you'll be detained uninjured and set off at the first port possible. But if I discover you, or if you commit an act of sabotage and are discovered, I'll personally find the most hideous means of dying possible for you—I swear it!''

Frost let loose of the trigger on the handle of the bullhorn and handed it to Timmons, saying, "Dismiss the men."

Walking toward the bow rail, Frost stopped, staring out to sea over the calm waters—he saw something. "Binoculars— Blackie," Frost snapped, starting toward the wheelhouse, Torres meeting him in the doorway, handing Frost the glasses. Frost brought the tubes to his eye, not bothering to adjust the left one. There were ten cutter like ships coming toward them at speed.

Marina was beside him them, saying, "Let me see," and Frost handed her the glasses. "Madre de dios," she whispered.

"What is it?" Frost asked her.

"I can see the flag—they are gunboats sent by Ramon, from Monte Azul."

Frost snatched back the glasses, stared, trying to focus on the moving object at the stern of the nearest boat—a purple and black flag with a single star over a hammer and sickle—the flag of the Communist Government of Ernesto Ramon.

Frost dropped the glasses to his side, turned and looked toward Blackie Torres, Torres already speaking, his voice low, "We cannot outrun them, even if we were already underway."

Frost let out a long, low sigh, leaning heavily

against the bow rail and staring at the dots of the ten ships, growing larger it seemed by the second. "Then we unlimber the deck gun, the M-79 grenade launchers—we fight!" He felt like adding, 'Damn the torpedoes and full speed ahead' but decided it was no time for levity.

Chapter Seven

As Frost summoned manpower for the deck gun and the grenade launchers to supplement it, the men ranking Captain or above were already beginning to assemble on the foredeck and Frost delayed the meeting, instructing the men to find their best riflemen from both ships and assemble them on the main decks of Angels One and Three, ready to move to whichever side was needed when firing began. Marina worked in the makeshift armory issuing weapons and ammunition as Frost positioned the deck gunners and gave them their orders—no firing unless fired upon, otherwise await his signal to open up.

Frost ran back to the bow rail. Looking through the glasses to get better detail, he shouted back to Blackie, "How long before they intercept?"

"Three, maybe four minutes, Captain Frost."

"Gotchya," Frost returned. "Timmons," he shouted.

"Sir," the Britisher answered, almost frightening Frost because he was so near.

Turning to the man, Frost said, "Hustle together anything passing for scuba gear, some good fighting knives and ten Greaseguns, spare magazines loaded and plastic trash bags—on the double."

"Very good sir," and Timmons saluted, Frost shaking his head as he returned it. As he took the glasses again, Frost swept the horizon—there were more ships coming, up from the starboard side of Angel Three. Frost focused in on them—"Damn," he rasped, dropping the glasses a moment, running his left hand through his hair, then scratching his stubbled chin. "Mexican coastal patrols . . ."

Frost handed off the glasses to Blackie, standing beside him now, running back toward the wheelhouse, shouting to Torres, "We're still in international waters, right?"

"Aye—what is—"

"Never mind," Frost rasped, reaching the wheelhouse, swinging inside and accosting the radioman—it was the same, thin featured younger man from the previous day. "What's your name," Frost snapped.

"Bessington."

"Okay—get me that Mexican gunboat fleet

out there—identify us as Angels One and Three out of wherever and remind them these are international waters, then ask their intentions. If you have to, tell them the story about Angel Two last night—just leave out the sabotage part and don't mention we're armed.''

Frost ran from the wheelhouse, shouting to the gunners assembling on the afterdeck, ''Cover that deck gun, keep those M-79s out of sight,'' then Frost snatched up the bullhorn, shouting through it to the deck of Angel Three, ''This is Frost—keep the riflemen out of sight—no weapons visible—move it.''

Holding onto the bullhorn still, Frost ran back to the bow rail, not needing the glasses anymore to spot the Communist armada approaching them, full detail possible because they were so close. He felt Marina's hand on his arm, glanced at her, then looked back seaward. ''What are they doing—why aren't they shooting?''

''They don't want a war with Mexico—I think. They were friendly to you before, the Mexicans—look over there,'' and Frost handed her the glasses and pointed to the dozen or so Mexican gunboats coming up on the side of the Angel Three.

''Sir,'' and Frost turned around. It was Timmons.

''What—you got it all?''

''Yes, sir!''

''Jees, man—you're gonna give yourself a sore throat with all that shouting,'' Frost cracked, good naturedly, slapping the man on the shoulder and adding, "Good job. Now find me nine volunteers with some scuba experience—best men you can."

"Eight volunteers, sir—S.A.S., sir—in case the Captain has forgotten."

Frost shook his head, "Hardly forget that, would I—nine volunteers—you run the show while I'm away." Frost started to turn to Marina, but already she was starting to speak. He cut her off. "You keep our Mexican friends entertained—I'm taking a party of nine men and myself over the side, out to meet the Monte Azulian armada or whatever—while they have fits over the Mexicans out here, we're going to give them a little reception. Be cool," and, without waiting for the girl to say anything, Frost started toward the main deck, jumping half the way down, already stripping away his pistol belt and boots.

"Timmons," Frost shouted, skinning out of his pants and fatigue blouse.

"Sir," and Frost turned as the Britisher bounded over.

"Look—keep Marina talking with the Mexicans, don't return fire on the Monte Azulian gunboats unless they open up and you need to—keep it as limited as you can. I'm taking your volunteers—where the hell are they?"

"Coming, sir," and Timmons turned, shouting, "Frogman team—front and center!"

Frost kept on talking, "I figure the Commies won't start shooting while the Mexicans are off our bows, and the Mexicans won't shoot at all.

Until the Commies get up their nerve, we've got some time. I'm taking the scuba team around behind them, underwater as far as we can and we're boarding two of the ships, then turn their own guns on them—then you give the order here for our guys to open up and let 'em have it—okay?''

"Very good sir," and Timmons turned again, "Frogmen team—front and center! Damnit!''

Less than a second after Timmons shouted, the first of the men appeared from below deck, carrying two Greaseguns with him and the armful of plastic trashbags Frost had ordered.

"Good," Frost rasped, getting to his feet, pulling up the straps on the nearest of the air tanks, not bothering with more than a glance at the pressure gauge. Ripping his webbed belt from his fatigue trousers he lashed it around his waist, clipping one of the M-16 bayonets on it before closing the belt. He pulled on the diving mask, the fins already in place. The equipment was old, the rubber foul smelling even before putting the mouthpiece to his face.

He snatched up a Greasegun, checked the actions, rammed a magazine in place and stuffed the loaded subgun and three extra magazines into one of the plastic bags, knotting the bag.

By now, the rest of the nine volunteers were assembled, all had virtually completed suiting up. "All right," Frost began. "We go over the side, swim together underwater, come up from behind the two nearest boats, we take 'em.''

"Why not the center boats, sir?'' The voice

belonged to a red-haired kid.

"Then once we started shooting at them, they could all shoot at us. This way only one or two of their boats will be able to return fire without fear of hitting their own people—right?"

"Yes, sir," the red-haired boy answered.

"Good—you lead the second team—consider it a field promotion for initiative—that'll teach you to shut up," Frost added, smiling. "No time for questions—let's go! Everybody know how to swim?"

Frost didn't wait for an answer, instead pulling his mask down and putting his mouthpiece in place and going to the railing. He gave Timmons a parting slap on the shoulder, stepped over the railing and jumped, the impact against the water with the weight of the tanks awkward. Pulling below the surface, Frost started treading water as the other nine men impacted near him. Using hand signals, Frost designated four men to be his team, four for the red-haired questioner, then started swimming toward the stern of Angel One.

The water was warm, almost unpleasantly warm in the situation, the kind of temperature that made you want to sit back, close your eyes and sleep. And, with virtually no sleep in two days, Frost was exhausted. He kept moving through the water, using his feet as much as possible to propel him, arms at his sides, the plastic bag with the Greasegun in it dragging at his right side in the water.

Reaching the stern of the Angel One and signalling the other men to stay below, Frost sur-

79

faced, orienting himself on the Monte Azulian ships just off the bow in an uneven rank blocking the bows of the Angels One and Three. Frost picked the two ships he wanted, hitched at his underpants sagging under the weight of the water and ducked down below the surface again, signalling the nine other men to follow him. He wanted the two Communist gunboats on the far side of Angel Three, nearest the Mexican gunboats, further impeding return fire once Frost and his men took over the two boats and opened up. Gliding behind the stern of Angel Three they swam underwater along the starboard side, Frost able to see the faint outline of the nearest of the Mexican gunboats in the water to his right.

As they moved, Frost glanced about him, assessing the men—none of them seemed to be any wonder as a swimmer, but despite the disguise of the masks and scuba gear they wore, there was a set to their faces—he felt good about them. Even with the bow of the Angel Three, Frost signalled to the red-head, pointing out the second ship and the red-head acknowledging, Frost taking his men toward the outline of the nearest Communist gunboat, the rumble of its engines clear now through the water, Frost unlimbering the knife at his hip as he touched the hull, the other four men around him.

Putting the knife into his teeth pirate fashion, Frost ripped through the plastic bag, snatching at the Greasegun, shoving the three spare magazines he'd taken into the belt cinched around his waist. Ducking down under the surface, he loosed the tanks from his back, kicking away the flippers, undoing the weight belt, the other four doing the same. His head broke the surface on the portside of the craft, and Frost threw away the mask, the subgun slung across his chest and he reached up and shoved himself over the gunwales, the other four behind him.

"Usted esta rodeado por mios soldados," Frost shouted, already opening fire, the .45 caliber subgun bucking in his hands as he ran across the narrow deck almost cutting the aft deckgunner in half as he tried wheeling the machinegun he manned toward Frost, Frost rolling clear of the blast his deathgrip made, one of Frost's four men catching it. "Get forward," Frost shouted, then collared one of his men and half threw him toward the machinegun.

Gunfire—small arms, handgun and subguns were opening up, two men coming up from the cabin, shooting, Frost and some of his men firing back. Frost jumped up onto a narrow catwalk-like way around the cabin on the portside, edging forward, the machinegun on the bow still silent, but subgun fire pouring aft toward him. His underpants falling down because the elastic was wet, Frost crouched, tugged at them, then edged forward again, a subgunner rushing him, Frost firing his gun empty now, the man still moving, Frost's left hand flashing up, snatching the bayonet and flipping it in mid-air to catch the handle, then underhanding it forward into the subgunner's guts, Frost ramming a fresh magazine into the Greasegun and continuing to fire, already exchanging shots.

"Where the hell are you, Red," Frost shouted, not seeing the boy who led the second commando team. But then, from the corner of his eye, coming up on the stern of the second gunboat, Frost saw him, the subgun in his hands firing, but firing seaward as the other four men clambered over behind him, gunning them down, kicking one man back into the water.

Frost ducked, a burst of submachinegun fire ripping into the outside cabin bulkhead beside him, his own gun firing, answering, killing the last of the men at the bow of the gunboat he was aboard. He saw the red-haired kid's lips moving, unable to hear the words over the din of gunfire, but suddenly the crew of the second ship was joining with him, firing toward the ship where Frost and the two survivors of his men were.

"Son of a," Frost started, firing his Greasegun over the roof of the cabin, then running forward, trying for the machinegun mounted at the bow. There was a burst of subgun fire, and Frost dropped to the deck, his left leg feeling as though it were on fire, but Frost rolled, the subgun in his own hands coming up, firing, the red-haired kid standing on the roof of the cabin on the next gunboat, wild look in his blue eyes, fire pouring from the greasegun he held in his fists. "Last time I'll go for apple pie and motherhood," Frost rasped, his trigger finger already twitching at the Greasegun in his own hands, Frost and the red-head firing, Frost feeling a slug or two—he wasn't sure—tear at his left side, but his finger still squeezing the trigger. Both guns emptied almost simultaneously, Frost and the red-haired kid staring at one another, then the red-head moved the subgun from in front of him—his stomach was a mass of ragged red blotches and he doubled over and fell from the cabin roof, out of sight between the two gunboats. "Now Timmons," Frost shouted, pushing himself to his feet, slipping on his wounded left leg, crashing to his knees, then pushing himself up again. Frost reached the machinegun, started wheeling it, already finding the double triggers, his fist clenched on them, then compressing them. The massive machinegun fired, the rhythm slow by comparison to the Greasegun, the slugs hammering into the cabin of the next gunboat, from the corner of his eye Frost seeing the two survivors of his men crowding near him, their Greaseguns firing. Frost almost stopped firing, turning his head, looking to his left—"Thunder?" But it was the deck gun, he saw, and the grenadiers were firing as well, the first shell from the deck gun impacting on the third gunboat, from where Frost fought, a belching up of flame following it in the center of the gunboat's deck. Frost kept firing the machinegun, two shots nailing into the lead man of a party of Communists coming toward the gunboat, on foot, jumping the narrow gaps of water between each of the boats, as the deck gun on Angel One fired again.

Frost kept firing, grenades landing on the Communist gunboats, explosions everywhere.

83

Frost spotted the man he pegged as the Commander of the Armada, in the fourth boat from him—something about the man's face, the carriage, the orders he was barking that Frost could not hear—Frost could only see the lips moving.

"Here," Frost shouted, grabbing one of his men and shoving the man toward the gun. Frost grabbed the man's Greasegun, fired it out in a long burst and rammed a fresh magazine in place, then started running, his left hand hitching up his sagging underpants, his wounded left leg burning as he jumped to the deck of the next boat. From the corner of his eye as he looked seaward he could see lifeboats coming, grenadiers on them, firing, and Frost kept running, dodging, firing. He wanted the Commander.

A Communist crewman was running toward Frost as Frost jumped to the deck of the third gunboat and Frost fired, missing, then snapping the skeletonized wire stock of the M-3 out, bending it as it impacted against the man's head. Frost dropped to the deck, the machinegun in the bow of the fourth ship firing, but in an instant there was a flash and Frost covered his head with his hands, then looked up, a grenade having hit the gun emplacement. Frost snatched at the Greasegun on the deck beside him, pushed himself to his feet and ran, jumping the gap between the third and fourth gunboat, landing hard on the deck.

Sweeping the gun in a fast arc, Frost spotted the man he wanted—the Commander of the gunboats, edging out of sight on the far, starboard side of the gunboat's cabin. Frost fired, high, ripping at the wood and glass, then running.

Frost reached the cabin, stopped, firing the Greasegun from his left hand around the side of the exterior bulkhead, an answering burst chewing into the cabin wood beside him. Frost fired again, then waited, another answering burst. This time Frost dove around the outside corner of the cabin, going flat out on the narrow walkway a burst of automatic weapons fire zinging over his head, his own M-3 firing, Frost kneecapping the Commander, the man collapsing back and off the cabin level onto the deck below. Frost pushed himself to his feet, ran three steps and jumped, diving down, onto the Communist Commander, the Greasegun clattering to the deck as Frost hammered his already battered right fist into the Communist Commander's face. The man was screaming from the knee wounds and Frost grabbed at him, finding the Greasegun and jabbing the stubby muzzle against the man's nose, rasping, in ungrammatical Spanish, "Totoalos hombres manos ariba, vaminos," and Frost jabbed the muzzle of the Greasegun into the Communist Commander's left nostril, blood spurting from it. The man stopped screaming, then shouted.

"Soy Dominguez—Baje sus armas—alto la fuega!"

"Manos arriba, tambiene," Frost rasped, giving the gun muzzle a twist.

"Manos arriba—ahora!" the bleeding, ghostly pale Communist Commander almost screamed.

Frost shouted in English, "Timmons—cease fire!" Then again, the volume of gunfire already subsiding, "Timmons—cease fire." Frost got back to his knees, holding the Greasegun now some inches from the Communist Commander's head. The gunfire had died, and around him Frost could see the Communist gunboat crewmen dropping their weapons, raising their hands. Frost looked back to the Communist Commander—there was a small pistol, a .25 in his bloodied right hand. Frost guessed the reason, rasping, "Dejela caer!"

The man eyed the gun, then with a look of despair in his pain-widened eyes, he let the weapon sink from his hand to the deck, clattering against it. "Tiene usted un doctor?" Frost asked, again feeling his Spanish sounded like it belonged to a slow first grader.

"No," the man murmured.

Frost nodded, saying, "Nosotros tenemos," and in English he shouted, "Timmons!"

Surprisingly clearly, he heard from across the water on the deck of Angel One, "Sir!"

"More medics—on the double—they don't have their own!"

"Yes, sir!"

Frost turned, staring down at the Communist Commander, now beginning to feel the pain of his own leg wound and the near miss creases along the left side of his rib cage. Feeling slightly stupid kneeling in a pool of blood on the gunboat deck holding a subgun and wearing nothing more than his underpants, Frost leaned forward slightly, "Yo hablo Espanol mal—quantos personas estuven in mes soldados—ahora," and Frost punched the muzzle of the Greasegun forward.

The man, the pale skin color turning almost green, whispered, barely audibly, "Dos hombres."

"El ninio con el pelo roho," Frost asked, the boy with the red hair?

"Si?"

"La otra? La otra?"

"Allemagne—Grunwald."

"Gracias," Frost sighed—Grunwald and the red-haired man had been the two. He pushed himself to his feet, the first of his men boarding the ships. He collared one of the men with a medical kit and aimed toward the Communist Commander. At the top of his lungs, he shouted, "Who speaks Spanish?"

Two or three of the men from the Angel One started to turn around. Frost picked one—a blonde-haired guy about thirty-five, "Take charge here—get these people underway on as many boats as they need to carry them, scuttle the ones that aren't salvageable, man the others for us—scrounge all the weapons, maps, codebooks—the whole bit. Make sure the medical attention is the best we can provide."

Frost heard another voice behind him and turned, the man saying, "Why—they wouldn't for us."

"Yeah, well," Frost began, already limping

away, "if we were them, what the hell would we be fighting for anyway?"

Enigmatic always sounded intelligent, he thought.

Chapter Eight

The Mexicans had said nothing afterward, the apparent Commander of the fleet of gunboats silently saluting across the water separating Angels One and Three from the guardian angel Mexicans as the two freighters steamed out farther into international waters. Frost, his leg wound bandaged, his side treated with antiseptic, sat on the forward deck, by the bow rail, watching the sun go down again—he was determined to sleep that night. Marina came up beside him and Frost looked up at her, saying, "I'm sacking out in about ten minutes—let me sleep as long as you can before I keel over—catch that nautical term, huh," he smiled.

"Hank—you are—"

"I'm just Hank, kid—and lucky sometimes. We're changing course—I've already worked it with Blackie and the other skipper on Angel Three. Too long to explain, I'll run it by you tomorrow. Anyway, these things are too big to get into coastal waters too close, those three gunboats we acquired won't help much—there's an island the French used to own—called Sabot."

"The Naval Base for Ramon's coastal guard?"

"Yeah," Frost sighed, dragging heavily on his cigarette watching the sunset. "Well, most military terms come from the French during their empire days with Napoleon. Like bayonet—from Bayonne. Same with Sabotage—had some saboteurs who worked at a shoe factory or something like that—sabot means shoe, I remember," Frost said, his speech sounding slurred and drunken to him and he hadn't consumed alcohol for days. Maybe that was the problem, he thought. "Well—Sabot, that island, sounds like a perfect place for some sabotage of our own, doesn't it—now help me get to bed and whatever you do don't forget to pour me a drink—I'm so tired I won't get to sleep otherwise," He started to his feet, having agreed earlier to use Marina's cabin, which had previously been Blackie's cabin. As he stood, swaying a little from the wound and the exhaustion, he felt the girl lean up and kiss him.

"We'll" make it, kid," he smiled, bracing his right arm across her shoulders.

"I know we will—I wasn't thinking that."

He smiled, "Yeah, well—not that I'm turned off to girls or anything, but I'm so tired I can't," he smiled again, holding her closer.

"I know," she whispered.

Silently the rest of the way, she helped Frost below deck and to her cabin, pulling off his pants and boots and shirt for him, pouring a tumbler half full of Seagrams Seven. Frost took a healthy gulp and lay back. "You wake me if anything . . ."

Frost opened his eyes and it was just nearly dark through the porthole. He stared at his watch in the half light, unable to read the date on the Omega, then pushed himself stiffly up on his elbows, pulled the chain on the light over the bunk or berth—he'd never make a sailor, he decided. While he had to go to the bathroom and tried figuring out whatever you called it, he'd . . . He squinted against the light from the lamp and read the date, then the time on the Omega—either he'd slept forty-five minutes or nearly twenty-four hours—he decided on the latter, felt his stubbled face and decided the added growth confirmed the twenty-four hour figure. He tried to stand up, leaned back again and stared about the cabin.

"Ahh," he muttered, getting to his feet. The cabin had its own bathroom. He walked a little unsteadily to it, did what he had to and then studied his face in the smudged mirror, shaking his head to clear it. He'd fallen asleep with his eyepatch on, hadn't shaved in so many days his mustache and sideburns were starting to blend in with his beard and his eye was hollow, sunken looking. He decided the latter was dirt and he turned on the tap, splashed water on his face and then remembered to remove the patch. He threw it away—he had more. There was a shower and he checked that it worked, although there wasn't any warm water. He stripped off his underpants and climbed in, washed his body and his hair and stood under the water a while. He tried remembering all that had happened. After the battle for the gunboats, his wounds dressed, "Ouch," he rasped as he touched accidentally against his left rib cage. He looked down. The grazes seemed clean enough. He looked at the packing over the leg wound. It had been changed while he'd slept—probably Marina—he seemed to remember something about that and it involved Marina. He'd showered in the cabin after the battle—that's right, he thought. That was why the shampoo was there, and he remembered noticing his razor.

He shut off the water and stepped out, found a clean-looking towel and dried off, then took the razor and plugged it in. "Damn," he snapped at himself, remembering to pop the plastic blade cover off the Norelco again, then starting once more to scrape at the stubble. He used an electric razor whenever possible, using a safety only in the field. Where there was electricity available, forget it, he had long ago determined.

He licked his tongue over his teeth, the sensation terrible, found his kit and the toothbrush and toothpaste and dental floss and gave himself the works, gargling with a mouthful of the whiskey from the bottle beside the bed and spitting it into the sink.

Near the mound of his things that Marina had insisted he store there were the cammie fatigues he'd worn and gotten sodden during the fire—all of his things, apparently, had been washed. He started to search for underpants and socks when he stopped, reaching for the High Power still in the belt holster beside the bunk, the door opening into the cabin. Frost relaxed and put the High Power back—it was Marina.

"Hey kid—shouldn't have let me sleep so much, but I'm glad you did—felt almost human again."

"We'll be nearing the coast of Monte Azul in three hours—I thought you might want to eat, whatever before then so I came to wake you."

"Come here," Frost told her, the girl coming over to the bunk and sitting down beside him.

"Wait," she said then, standing again, "you have me at a—what is the word—disadvantage, no?"

Frost looked at her, "I'm still a little fuzzy, what?"

"Here," and Frost watched as she undid the buttons on the blue work shirt she wore with her right hand, the fingers of her left hand tugging down the zipper on her jeans. "Are you awake enough now?"

"Yeah, well," Frost started. "As a matter of fact—"

He stopped talking, watching her instead, the

93

shirt falling from her shoulders to the cabin floor, the jeans dropping to her ankles. She stepped out of them. Wearing just her panties and a white bra, she walked to the cabin door, threw the bolt on it and turned around, somehow as she turned the bra coming undone and she leaned her shoulders downward, the straps falling from them, the bra falling to the floor. She stepped over it and kneeled up on the bed beside Frost. He leaned back, watching her, feeling her lie beside him, his eye closed a moment.

His right arm caught up the hair at the nape of her neck. He opened his eye and crushed his lips on hers, his left hand reaching down, struggling the panties from her hips and down along her thighs. "You should wear socks," he muttered, "could be bad for your feet. And barefoot you could get planters warts maybe," he told her.

"You never stop," she sighed. "Tell me an eyepatch story—like in old times, bueno?"

"Okay," he laughed, kissing her neck, "Well, I was in Germany you see—not much of a story really. Commando type operation, well . . . There was this German farmer and we had to cross his property to get to the objective—going after some terrorist we were, part of a NATO thing. Well, I was the Commander and I asked the farmer what was beyond the little wooded area just on the other side of the fence. Well, you know how rotten I am with language and everything . . ." and Frost moved his left hand to the insides of her thighs. "Well, the farmer didn't speak much English and we fooled around with sign language and everything and he finally said, "Mein field," and I said, "Well, good for you—and I suppose that's your stand of trees too," then I patted him on the back and we marched off. Got to the other side of the trees. Well, my dumb mistake. Good thing I went first. I was the only one injured," and Frost buried his face in her neck.

"How—your eye," she laughed.

"Well, see I thought the farmer had said, 'Mein field.' Well, he'd really said—"

The girl cut him off, a healthy, throaty woman's laugh coming from her, "Mine field, correcto?"

"Si, ninia," Frost murmured, choking off the laughter as he kissed her mouth, their tongues touching briefly, hot, hers darting against his. He slid between the warmth of her thighs, his left hand now against the nipple of her right breast, feeling her hands on him. There was a pounding in his body and he moved against her, felt her hands and then they were gone, moistness surrounding him, warmth. His right hand arched up her back, her abdomen tight against him. "Hank," she whispered.

Chapter Nine

"When my father ruled," Marina said, standing beside him on the rear deck of the Angel One, watching the almost luminous waters of their wake in the darkness, "the island of Sabot was a nature preserve—like the Galapagos a little. But this bastard Ramon," and she shook, Frost pulling her closer to him. She wore one of Frost's fatigue blouses over her shirt, the sleeves rolled up but her hands still half lost in them.

Her dark hair tossed by the wind, Frost looked at her, watching her features in the semi-darkness of the quarter moon and the stars. "Give me a drink, Hank," she murmured.

Frost reached into his hip pocket and produced the small flask, one handed it open and passed it to her. She tossed her head back, drinking, then handed it back to him. Frost took a swallow, then closed it, looking at her again. "You hate Ramon personally, don't you?"

"Why should I not—como no?"

"Well, if it hadn't been him it would have been some other Communist macho type they would have shoved in. Hell, Ramon's probably scared to death of us by now," and Frost and the girl both laughed.

He turned her around, holding her full in his arms. The spray was whipping up as the wind increased off the stern and Frost pulled the girl to him, kissing her, her mouth moving under his, her tongue searching him. Then her face was beside his, her chin against his chest as he bent over her, her mouth beside his right ear. She was whispering. "I have never met a man like you—you are fierce, you are gentle, you are a killer, you are compassionate—how do I know you?"

"Shut up," he told her, knotting the finger of his left hand into the almost black hair at the nape of her neck, forcing her mouth under his kissing her, feeling her body press against him, surrendering against him. They stood on the stern deck a while longer before the cold and the knowledge that they would soon be nearing Sabot brought the world back—Frost sometimes wished the world would go away for good.

She kept him company in the galley, drinking coffee only as Frost devoured two plates of beef with sunnyside up eggs and tomato slices added

97

on top. He took the last slice of apple pie, poured himself a third cup of coffee and slowed down, talking with Marina, not caring if the cook overheard. As he pushed the emptied metal pie plate aside, Frost lit a Camel, saying to her, "I don't remember how much I told you before I took that sleep—I was beat out," Frost began. "I decided a couple of things, then gave Blackie and the Captain of Angel Three the orders to make the course corrections—we draw too much water—even as a guy who knows the proverbial stuff from shoe polish about boats and ships and stuff, I know we can't get close enough to shore to get in without getting polished off by Ramon's guns. So, we go to Sabot."

"But the island is a fortress—it was a pirate stronghold during the—"

"I know," Frost smiled. "And how Ramon had fortified the place, took over the town and turned it into a barracks moving out the natives that didn't go along. I know the whole thing—I did my homework before taking the job. That doesn't change anything. You, with Timmons helping you are going to begin a naval bombardment of the main town. I'm taking a couple hundred guys through the jungle with me from the back end of the island. He's got a much smaller base there. We're going to time the bombardment for just about when we reach the town."

"A bombardment—We cannot—"

"Relax," Frost said. "This may not get studied at West Point but it'd make a hell of a 1930s movie anyway. Like Sir Francis Drake and all those other guys—we can't take the main town, so we're setting up a fake naval bombardment. We cut across the island and while they're so busy laughing at your bombardment they can't take their eyes off the sea, I lead my force against them from the land. With a little luck and the element of surprise, we got it knocked —maybe.''

"What?"

"Yeah—would I joke?"

They both laughed. "Anyway," Frost smiled, "I always liked playing pirate when I was a kid," and he tugged at the eyepatch. "Here—I got a drawing of it somewhere," and Frost fished in his pockets, found his notebook and pulled it out. He lit another cigarette and flipped through the pages. "No—not this—what girl," he cracked.

"Oh—be quiet Hank," she laughed.

"Get me some coffee, kid, huh?" Frost asked, looking up at her then back to the notebook. He stopped, flipped back a few pages and turned the book around to her as she sat down again, putting the coffee in front of him. "It looked better before the notebook got all wet the other day," he told her.

The notebook page had a drawing resembling a crude, huge, long and narrow shoe—hence the name Sabot as Frost had explained, "Now," he said, pointing toward the right side of the shoe toward the heel, "this is the town of Genevieve—knew a girl by that name once—I wouldn't want to meet a dame like that again if you paid me. Anyway, we hit Genevieve right in the butt end," and the girl laughed, "then I push on through the jungle along the arch of the shoe, so to speak, toward the big toe area, the town of Normandie—Normandy invasion right? You begin your bombardment—we'll co-ordinate the times later just prior to the operation. See, I'm going ashore with a raiding party of maybe four hundred men—take the town of Genevieve really quick, then we load only half as many men out, while I slip into the jungle with my people. If the Commander of Normandie down here," and Frost pointed to the crude drawing of Sabot, "hears of the invasions, he'll assume most of the survivors pulled out. If he's the really cautious type then he'll send out patrol boats along the beach—he'd never think anybody in his right mind would head across the jungle—supposed to be like Panama in there—swamps, everything. When he doesn't see anyone on the beach but instead sees you steaming nice and slowly toward Normandie, he'll set up to repel your bombardment or another beach assualt. We get through, sack the quarterback when he isn't looking."

"Tu es—ahh, English," the girl snapped. "You are crazy—loco. You will be killed."

"Sounds good to you, too, huh?" Frost leaned forward and held her hand, looking into her eyes by the galley lamp swinging overhead with the movement of the ship. He tongued the Camel into the left corner of the mouth, the smoke curling up toward his eyepatch.

"Pirate," she laughed.

Chapter Ten

Frost ran the details by again, but to himself. Normandie was on the toe side of the shoe, facing Monte Azul, and here on the far, heel side, there was no reason to expect terrible resistance in the small town of Genevieve. Frost remembered the woman who had worked for the neo-Nazis in Paris, betrayed him to torture, tried gouging his other eye out before he'd broken her neck* . . . Genevieve—a lovely name—he hoped he liked the little island town better.

They had scrounged every rubber boat, lifeboat—anything that would float to get the three hundred and eighty-five men through the water and toward the beach five miles off from Genevieve. It was going in several rotations and on the last the boats would be hauled back and taken aboard the Angel One and Angel Three

*See They Call Me The Mercenary #3, FOURTH REICH DEATH SQUAD.

and Marina and Timmons and the best of the marksmen and the bulk of the mercenary force would steam slowly around the island toward the bombardment of Normandie and Ernesto Ramon's naval station.

Frost's Avon inflatable hit the beach and Frost jumped out into the surf, running in a low crouch through it—like the previous night when he and Marina had stood in the stern of Angel One, the moon was bright and so were the stars. The CAR-16 in his right hand, the Browning strapped to his right hip, his own two Gerber knives—the small Mk I and the Mk II fighting knife—hung from his trouser belt, a bayonet from the pistol belt, the Interdynamics KG-9 pistol slung from a makeshift webbing off his chest. Using hand signals, he drew the men in toward the shore, watching for the signal for the previous party—each used a different series of lights to avoid a trap—and he headed the party of men toward it.

There were already two hundred men in the trees and shrubs rimming the white sanded beach and Frost dropped to the sand beside those of his operational commanders already in place, then he waited. He lit a Camel, staring out over the water, watching the boats going back to bring another landing party. He checked the luminous black face of the Omega Seamaster 120 on his left wrist. The operation was, so far, seven minutes ahead of schedule. Frost automatically checked his weapons.

Another hour passed and all three hundred eighty-five men were in place. Two hundred of the men carried empty packs stuffed with old laundry or

102

anything to bulge them out. Frost and one hundred eighty four others carried two days rations, extra water, snakebite kits, extra ammo and explosives— enough to make the estimated twenty-six hour trek down the center of the island to attack Normandie.

Toward the last, ten minutes before they were to move out, Frost called the commanders together. "I'm not running things by you guys again—we all know the drill inside out—but we're not supposed to do it that way," and the assortment of operational commanders laughed. "Now—we get in there, take the place as quickly as possible then start operation attrition—right back into the jungle. We all rendezvous where we pre-arranged and get going—faster time we make the less time we have to walk in that jungle at night—which is the only crazy part. One more thing," Frost cautioned. "Prisoners. I don't particularly want any, but any we get can stay with the residual force I'm leaving to hold the town," Frost resisted saying 'hold Genevieve'. "I don't want prisoners summarily shot."

"Why the good guy crap, Frost?"

"Because I like to sleep at night, Creston," Frost answered, glaring at the man's silhouette in the moonlight. "When I was in Africa, there were guys who got their rocks off torturing people, killing prisoners—I won't say they were any of my guys. We've all seen it. If that turns you on, terrific—you won't mind my killing you when I see you or one of your men doing it. This is a war—not an SS reunion. Remember that."

Frost waited a moment. Then, "Any questions?" No one said anything and Frost said, "All right—

103

let's move people out," and he looked at the Omega, "three minutes. Have your guys make sure all their men have sling swivels taped, the whole nine yards, all the good commando stuff—move out," and Frost sat back in the sand as the operations commanders left. He wished he hadn't left Timmons back on the boat. And, he made a mental note to dislike Creston.

Frost and his men moved out, hugging the beach as much as they could toward the small town and the small naval base, hoping, Frost felt they all did, that the naval base was as small as it seemed to be from what Frost felt were laughingly called "intelligence sources." He had checked ten news magazines, a travel encyclopedia and back issues of various wildlife and geographic publications on the ruination of the natural habitat the exotic island animals had suffered since the naval bases were set up to expand Monte Azul's territorial waters 150 miles out into the Pacific.

It took less than an hour—again ahead of schedule—for Frost's force to reach the perimeter of the town—the 'outskirts of Genevieve' they had all laughed before. Frost, with a dozen men, lay back as his operations commanders moved their men into position around the town, waiting. Frost checked his watch. Sunrise would be in fifty eight minutes if the almanac he'd checked was correct.

Frost passed the words for weapons checks and total silence otherwise, then waited, now not daring a cigarette and wanting one badly. The jungle stopped abruptly outside the long street of the town, the naval installation at the far side by the small harbor.

Marina's ships would stop there, as they steamed along the island perimeter, to unload the two hundred men or how many actually survived. Frost stopped thinking about the plan. He tried to think about Bess, found he couldn't do that either because it reminded him of the one hundred thousand dollars he was getting paid for the job and that reminded him of the plan again.

He tried thinking about Marina, remembering each detail of her body as they had made love the previous night. He checked his watch. Frost wondered how it would go down with Commacho's nephew when they met—the young man blamed Frost, Marina had said, blamed Frost for killing his Uncle. Frost somehow had always felt that Commacho himself, bull of a man, the massive, good-humored soldier, would have understood, the exigency of war, all that stuff, Frost thought. If he had not derailed Commacho's military train the train would have pushed Aguillara-Garcia's train off the rails where it had itself crashed to avoid going off the destroyed bridge. Commacho would have understood. Frost checked his watch again. He hoped sunrise was early. There was a young man near him and Frost asked his name, "Hey—tell me about yourself."

"I'm Frank Carr, sir. I was a Corporal in the U.S. Army. I liked being a soldier, I didn't like the Army much though—kind of boring. So, here I am."

"What do you do," Frost asked the boy. "I mean, when you aren't doin' all this exciting stuff." He realized the kid made him feel old.

"Well—I'm a pretty good mechanic—you know

cars, trucks, motorcycles. I did that for a while in the Army, too, took a lot of shop courses in high school."

"Do you know how few American mercenaries there are, son?" Frost asked.

"Not too many, I know."

"Well—you just remember one reason there aren't more of them—I mean, there're a lot of reasons but this is a good one to remember."

"What's that, sir," the young man asked him.

"It's called death, kid—don't be a hero out there. You ever do this before?"

The boy didn't answer for a moment. Then, "No, sir—I read a lot about mercenaries, I wanted to try."

"Well, if you get home you can tell everybody you tried it—but you can't if you don't make it—remember that."

"But, sir?"

"What?" Frost whispered, the darkness starting to turn grey now. He checked his watch.

"Nothing, I guess, sir."

"What?" Frost repeated.

"Well, sir, why do you do it, sir? I mean, be a mercenary."

"Me," Frost smiled. "Well, aside from the fact I don't have six weeks to fill you in, it's kind of hard to explain. I don't like the Communists—I mean, nothing personal against them. If they want to be Communists, good for them. I just don't like them trying to make everybody else be a Communist whether they like it or not. I learned how to fight, never stuck at much of anything else and fighting things I didn't like instead of just swallowing them always seemed like a better idea to me." Frost changed the subject. "You got a girl?"

"Yeah—I mean, yes, sir—name is Jill—I tell you, pretty."

"Yeah—me too, I got a girl," Frost told the boy.

"You mean the Senorita—I mean, we all kind of see you and her."

"Well that's a funny story—but I didn't mean her. But yeah, she and I are close. But I got a girl—named Bess. Pretty lady, too. I'll show you her picture when we get back," and Frost found his palms sweating. He realized suddenly that hours earlier on the other side of the world when this day had begun Bess had had the operation—whether she would be back to normal or be crippled for life had been decided. His stomach churned. She could handle the eye—Frost tugged at the eyepatch a moment. He wondered if he were able to handle things as well as she had.

"Could I ask a question, sir?"

Frost looked at the kid, then at his watch. It was nearly time for the attack to begin. "Yeah—what's the question?" but Frost already suspected it.

"I mean, sir—if it isn't too personal—the eyepatch. A lot of us have been wondering?"

"Well," Frost began, "not much of a story really. See, when I was about your age I had some free time and I drifted down to a candy store in the town I was stationed near. Always had a sweet tooth, if you know what I mean," and Frost laughed softly, "Well, the place specialized in taffy, saltwater taffy, the really sticky kind. Well, there was this sunlamp salesman in the store, buying himself some taffy. Guy who ran the place, old man Running Bear—"

"Running Bear, sir. Was he an Indian?"

"Got me," Frost said. "I always thought he was Norwegian—blonde hair, spoke with a kind of 'by-yumpin'-jiminy' accent. Anyway, old man Running Bear got kind of interested in the sunlamp the salesman was selling. I was buying some taffy, decided to look at the sunlamp too. Well, that's when the Fleischenheimer gang came in."

"The Fleischenheimer gang?"

"Yeah—jumped the reservation—Chippewas, I think they were. Bunch of juvenile delinquents, a real disgrace to their noble heritage as the First Americans, let me tell you," Frost said, checking his watch again. Almost time. "Well, the Fleischenheimer gang started talking rough and dirty—called old man Running Bear a foreigner and everything. Well, we all got to fighting. There were eight of them. The sunlamp salesman helped out—I guess he figures Indians wouldn't buy sunlamps anyway. Well, a big brawl broke out," and Frost glanced at his watch—he made it five minutes, give or take. "We were dukin' it out and, unbeknownst to me, well, my saltwater taffy had gotten under the sunlamp salesman's demonstrator model and begun melting. Pablo Fleischenheimer and I were fighting, rolling around on the floor and he got me down by the hand-dipped candy counter."

"Hand-dipped candy?"

"No—the counter. Anyway, suddenly Pablo reached up and tried to get away from me, push himself off because I was besting him, you see.

108

Well, his hand got stuck in the saltwater taffy and when he pulled on it he lost his balance, fell forward on me and his fist punched right into my left eye. I shoved him off—but when his fist came away, the one covered with all the taffy, well, my eye came—'' and Frost stopped, sniffing loudly.

"Then what, sir?" the kid asked.

"Then we attack," Frost rasped, reaching out the Heckler & Koch flare pistol from his pack, dropping a starburst red in and closing the action. He looked at the boy. "Remember, kid—no heroes, huh—go back to tell about it—to what's her name?"

"Jill, sir."

"Jill—pretty name—you're lucky," and Frost fired the flare, muttering under his breath, "God bless us—we're starting." Then pushing himself to his feet and flicking off the safety of the CAR-15 he started running forward, yelling, "Down with Ramon!"

Chapter Eleven

Frost ran forward, the ground covered with a light mist, gunfire erupting all around him as he started toward the street, his men already closing from both sides and swarming over the town and into the street ahead of him, gunfire coming too from the naval station at the far end of Genevieve where one hundred of Frost's men were concentrated to make a fast penetration and hold as the bulk of the force swept through the town to join up with them. The sunlight was streaming over the water now, casting long, almost supernatural shadows along the ground. Grenades exploded. Heavy machinegun fire still coming from the naval station ripped into the street and the adobe buildings fronting it, Frost and some of the men around him dodging toward the building for cover. There was an explosion then, from the naval station, the machinegun fire stopping. Frost shouted to his men, ''Let's go!'' and then started charging along the street, men joining him from the shelter of the buildings on both sides. Frost glanced beside and behind him—he was at the head of a pack of armed men numbering over a hundred, all of them shouting, some of them firing into the air. And suddenly, the shouting started blending together, two words clear on the morning air and Frost and the men of his company ran, ''Get Ramon!''

They were halfway down the length of the long street. ''Get Ramon!''

Soldiers, Ramon's troops or seamen, Frost wasn't sure, erupted from a building rooftop, firing a heavy caliber machinegun, some of Frost's men going down, Frost and some of the others dropping to their knees or flat on the ground and returning fire. Frost telescoped out the stock on his hybrid Colt rifle and with the selector at full auto began pumping three round bursts from the weapon toward the rooftop, nailing the man to Frost's right of the machinegunner, the man falling across the gun emplacement. There was a whooshing sound to Frost's left, then on the rooftop an explosion, the machinegun and the men around it flying in pieces through the air. ''Get Ramon!'' the chant started again.

Frost and the others around and behind him were up and running. As the sun winked higher over the horizon, Frost caught the glint of fresh sharpened bayonet cutting edges in the light. "Get Ramon!"

The naval station now dominated the end of the dust colored street, the last of the mist burning away as they charged the sunbleached building, the black and purple flag of the Communist Government of Monte Azul drooping from the pole atop the wall on the seaward side. "Get Ramon!" There was another explosion inside the naval station, a huge orange ball of fire and then a black puff of smoke belching high into the air, some shelling still pouring into the street toward Frost and his men. A mortar round whizzed overhead and the chanting stopped for a moment. Frost glanced around him—he had lost six men, but there was no stopping the charge, the chanting faster now, "Get Ramon! Get Ramon!"

"The sabotage on the boats?" Frost asked himself, the lives lost there, or maybe it was the "Angel" the boats were named after, or perhaps just a way of psyching up for the long, perilous assault through the jungle that lay ahead. "Get Ramon!" Frost heard himself shouting it too, now, "Get Ramon!"

They reached the end of the street and the outer wall of the naval station, still in a dead run, Frost and more than a dozen of the men flanking him almost simultaneously hitting the wall, jumping up and pulling themselves over, dropping down into the courtyard hand to hand fighting everywhere between Frost's advance force and the naval station defenders. Frost swung the CAR-16 into position, firing until the thirty round magazine was empty as he raced across the naval station parade ground.

Ramming another magazine in place, earing back the bolt and letting it fly forward, Frost and about thirty of his men, he judged, cut across the parade ground and toward the interior wall of the station.

Submachinegun fire was pouring down from the battlements above the ancient fortress now and Frost and his men dropped behind overturned vehicles, behind bodies of the fallen of both sides, returning fire to the gun position above them. "Get Ramon!" Frost shouted, then suddenly he was on his feet, a dozen or so men with him and they were running through the hail of gunfire toward the interior wall, hitting the wall, boosting one another over the top and up and Frost and a half dozen of his men dropped down beyond the interior wall, fighting there too hand to hand and deadly. Frost's CAR-16 was spitting three-round bursts of death almost like a living thing, Frost's hands holding and aiming and firing the gun almost as if they had minds of their own. And Frost's feet, moving swiftly across the interior courtyard, carried him too as if somehow the body and the mind had become detached, the body a fighting, killing machine and the mind only the observer rather than the master.

The CAR-16 ran dry and Frost, changing sticks, dodged to his left, one of the Communist defenders racing toward him, one of the newer Soviet AKM assault rifles in his hands, bayonet fixed. As the blade sliced through the air toward him, Frost dodged again, getting the fresh thirty-round magazine in place, working the bolt, the bayonet swiping toward him again. Frost fired, a three-round burst impacting laterally into the Communist's midsection, the man doubling over, turning on his toes and falling. Frost started moving across the courtyard again, the heaviest concentration of fighting at the base of a narrow, high tower. Frost glanced up, seeing why—that was where the purple and black Communist flag of Monte Azul flew from atop a pole. Frost raced toward the tower, firing at targets of opportunity, once one of the Communist fighters jumping Frost from the right side, Frost lashing out with the metal stock of the CAR and punching the man away. Frost reached the base of the tower, more than a dozen of his mercenary company fighting nearly twice that number of Communist forces from the naval station. One of Frost's mercs, one of the Englishmen with Timmons, had just rapped the butt of his M-16A1 into the jaw of one of the Communists. Recovering the weapon into a firing position, two Communist fighters started toward the Englishman.

No time to shout a warning, the men too close for Frost to shoot, Frost dove toward them, smashing outward with the butt of the Colt rifle in his hands, the butt hammering hard against the left temple of the nearer of the two men, Frost's left hand then reaching out, grasping the second man on the side of the face, pulling the Communist back. The hybrid assault rifle dangling from Frost's shoulder now, both hands free, Frost grabbed at the Communist's left ear with his right hand, turning the man around, his right hand already loosing the ear, drawing back and hammering forward, his fist balled, the already battered knuckles lacing across

114

the Communist's left jaw, knocking the man back. Frost started to wheel, grabbing for his rifle, two more Communists charging him. Frost lashed out with his left foot, a lethal savat kick impacting into the left ribcage of the nearer of the two attackers, Frost's left hand already grasping the big Gerber knife from his belt, tossing the knife through the air, catching it in his right hand as the second man lunged for him, Frost's rifle swinging out of the way across his back, the Communist's bayonet fitted assault rifle punching toward Frost's face. Sidestepping, Frost swung the double edged fighting knife in his right hand in a broad arc as the man hurtled past him, the point of Frost's knife slashing the right side of the Communist's neck, opening a broad, jagged gash there.

Streaming blood, the Communist wheeled, the bayonet held low, more like a short sword. As the Communist made his second lunge, Frost feigned a duplication of his last defense, starting to sidestep, to swing the knife in a broad, right handed arc. The Communist did a half-turn right, raising the rifle to catch the knife, Frost dodging back right, lunging forward with his fighting knife, like a swordsman, his legs angled forward, his right arm fully extended, his left out and behind him for balance. Frost's knife bit in under the breast bone and as Frost recovered from the lunge, he raked the blade down, opening the man, splitting him down the abdomen. As the Communist started to crumple to the ground, Frost had already wheeled away, the assault rifle coming back into his hands now as he fought his way toward the broad doorway at the base of the tower.

"Build your defense on me," Frost shouted, rallying the men of his force toward him.

The Communists ringed them, Frost and ten of his men with their backs to the tower, the Communists starting forward with fixed bayonets, Frost locking his own bayonet in place. Frost and the mercenaries of his force waited, crouched, their rifles held ready, the bayonet blades presented outward toward the advancing twenty or so of the enemy. As the Communists charged to close, Frost shouted, "now" and to a man, Frost's mercenaries opened fire, spraying their assault rifles on full auto, cutting the Communist fighters down into the dust.

"I'm getting that damned flag!" Frost shouted, starting into the tower entrance, then racing toward the narrow, rough stone steps, taking them three at a time as they wound upward. A bayonet punched out toward him, Frost falling back, nearly losing his balance, then his own rifle flashing outward, catching the blade of the Communist's bayonet, punching it aside, Frost's rifle driving forward into the neck of his opponent.

Stepping over the body, Frost started up the stairs again, changing magazines on the rifle he held. He froze against the near wall of the circular steps, bullets ripping into the stone of the far wall where his head had been seconds earlier.

Frost pushed the CAR-16 outward from him, trying to aim up the wall of steps, firing the weapon in full-auto, three-round bursts. There were more answering shots. Frost fired again, then when the answering burst came, Frost dove under it onto the steps, firing upward. There was a roar, a scream, then Frost was up, running up the steps three at a time, the Communist above him trying to recover his weapon into a firing position. Frost loosed a burst into the man's chest and stepped over him, racing to the top of the tower now.

The flagpole was just at the center of the tower landing, and Frost ran toward it, starting to undo the rope twisted around the turnbuckle at the base of the pole. Something inside him told him to dodge, and Frost wheeled, pulling left, a burst of automatic weapons fire cutting past him, some of the bullets impacting against the modern, hollow aluminum flagpole, the pole ringing loudly. Frost made to fire, loosed a three-round burst even before seeing his enemy, the man firing back, Frost glimpsing him as he ducked behind the opening leading to the steps going downward. Frost dove flat on the roof there, edging forward, another burst coming at him from the area beside the steps, then the Communist showing himself, running for the steps. Frost fired, missed, the CAR-16 empty. Pushing himself up, Frost ran, then dove toward the man, grabbing him, starting to wheel him around, Frost's right knee punching upward, catching the man in the groin, the knee punching up again, impacting under the man's down-thrusting chin, the Communist's head snapping up and back, his body lurching backward toward the edge of the roof, then falling out of sight.

There was a scream, almost inhuman, Frost thought. He ran toward the flagpole, undid the rope there and began hauling down the Communist flag of Monte Azul, the KG-9 pistol in Frost's left hand now and ready. Once the black and purple Communist banner was down on the roof, Frost undid it from the rope, reaching under his camouflage fatigue blouse, pulling out the folded flag there. Frost clipped the grommets to the rope, then started hauling it up. Before the flag had fully reached the top of the pole, there was a cheer. And as Frost lashed the rope to the turnbuckle and started toward the roof line, he looked down into the courtyard of the naval station and the two beyond. The fighting had essentially stopped, Communist troops were crawling out of defensive positions, hands in the air, Frost's men disarming them. And there were villagers, men and women and some children, the people of the town of Genevieve. Frost looked behind him, watched the free flag of Monte Azul blowing in the wind that had appeared almost magically in the bright sunlight. The cheering was growing louder.

Frost, the smile-frown lines on his face creasing into a grin, raised the Colt assault rifle high above his head and shouted, "Liberation!"

Chapter Twelve

Those surviving from the designated group of men who would press on overland toward Normandie had started filtering out of the street and the naval station yards and into the jungle almost as soon as Frost had raised the flag, and, himself having supervised the setup of a residual force to hold the town, Frost now pushed through into the jungle toward the rendezvous point, a dozen of his mercenary soldiers behind him.

They reached the rendezvous in twenty minutes, Frost saying nothing, just signalling the men to move out into the deeper jungle and toward the next battle. They moved throughout the rest of the morning hours in a brisk commando walk whenever the jungle growth wasn't too dense—time was their goal now—the less time spent trekking the jungle and the treacherous swamps to cross the island in darkness the better. Teams of men worked ahead of them with machetes, hacking clear a path where needed. Frost estimated he had 175 men—the young boy with the girl friend named Jill had made it and the realization of this made Frost glad. The teams of machete-wielding road clearers were replaced every half hour, the heat so intense, the humidity so great that any more prolonged period would have caused the men heat prostration, heart attack—and still the returning crews rejoining the column as it passed them were sweated through, pale, exhausted looking.

They pressed on past noon, Frost and his men snatching at food as they moved, pulling from their canteens to replace fluids they were losing from their bodies, popping salt tablets like candy.

By three P.M. they had crossed the low mountain range and its higher jungles and were entering the swamps—they were an hour ahead of schedule and Frost finally called the long, ragged, fanned out column to a halt. "Twenty minutes—pass it on," he rasped, then appointing men to stand perimeter watch, sending out the next machete team to replace the team already out there, their break time coming once they reached the previous road crew. Frost found a comfortable looking tree trunk and sat down on the mildly squishy ground, leaning back against the trunk, mopping his forehead, wringing out his crusher hat, popping two more salt tablets.

Frost turned, looking up, seeing young Corporal Carr walking past sitting, lying down, half collapsed men, and Frost rasped, "Here—over here!"

The boy turned, half smiling and started toward Frost, coming to attention, Frost waving him down, "Plant it—how you doin', Carr?"

"Fine sir—well, about as fine as anybody I guess. How much longer, sir?"

"Well," and Frost glanced at the Omega on his wrist. He smudged steam away from the outside of the crystal to read it with his right thumb. "I figure if we keep this pace, we should be in place by three, four A.M. maybe—let's say another twelve, thirteen hours—and that's good time."

"Then what?"

"Get some sleep, maybe two hours if we're lucky, then the attack on Normandie. At dawn, Marina's freighters are going to steam around into the harbor, the coupla gunboats we pirated off Ramon's people and what our guys scrounged back at the naval station at Genevieve—they all head for shore. Those heavy machineguns, the deck gun—all of it starts bombarding the Naval Station at Normandie while we come in from behind. Once we have things cookin', Timmons leads the amphibious assault force such as it is toward the town, we link up. Simple."

"What kind of a chance do we have, sir?" the boy asked.

Frost marvelled at his innocence, then looking the boy in the eye, answered, "Well—pretty good one, really. Our guys are going to be dead on their feet, but, we'll be fresh from a victory at Genevieve. There should be enough hype left to get the adrenalin flowing. They'll expect an attack from land, but I've got Timmons sending fifty men ashore on the beach five miles from Normandie to draw off some of Ramon's forces, keep them guessing. We've got a good chance, maybe even the losses won't be too heavy." Then lighting a cigarette, Frost asked. "You ever get in combat when you were in the Army?"

"No, sir," the boy said.

"You kill anybody this morning—I mean I know I shouldn't ask, but—"

"No, sir."

Frost slapped the boy on the shoulder, "Good for you, son."

"What?"

Frost looked at the boy, saying, "After this is all over, go home to that girl of yours—Jill?" Frost remembered the name perfectly well. "Tell everybody what a rough, tough mercenary you used to be and work on cars—smarter, believe me."

"But what about guys like you?"

"I don't know much about cars, kid," Frost smiled, pushing himself to his feet and shouting, "All-right. Pass the word . . . we're movin' out!" Frost looked down at Corporal Carr. "Remember what I said, son. Whether you wind up killing somebody or not in this thing tomorrow morning, then once we hit the beach at Monte Azul, whatever, get out. Otherwise, you're never going to marry that girl Jill, you're never going to be happy working on your cars, you're never going to—well," and Frost stubbed out his cigarette, "you'll just never do a lot of stuff. If there's a World War again, there'll be enough fighting to go around for everybody then. Just advice, take or leave it."

Carr got to his feet, saying. "But . . . I don't understand, sir."

"That's just the idea—if you keep doin' this, you'll get to understand," and Frost started walking away, shouting orders to his commanders.

Chapter Thirteen

There had been an "attack" by a snake fitting the size and general characteristics of an anaconda, but one of the island's local varieties, the creature nearly crushing the man it had gotten, Frost killing the thing with a machete. The swamp waters themselves had been filled with leeches and in the darkness, the mosquitoes and black flies had been in clouds, so thick Frost and the others had been able to move them apart in waves with their hands. One of the men had been bitten by something in the darkness, no one exactly certain what, though it had looked like a snake. He was feverish but as best as Frost or the medic could tell, he was in no imminent danger of death. The swamp itself had slowed them more than Frost had estimated and it was nearly five A.M. before they reached its end and started climbing again toward the small coastal plateau and the outskirts of the city, nearly six before they were able to stop in a ragged perimeter around the town of Normandie. The sky was already greying and Frost determined there was less than a half hour before the attack on the town had to begin. Too exhausted to be hungry, afraid to try grabbing a few minutes worth of sleep, Frost and his men made themselves as comfortable as they could, Frost studying the map of the town by a small pencil flash trying to determine if there should be any last minute changes in the attack plan, a scouting party sent ahead to infiltrate into the town and bring back any last minute intelligence. Frost smoked through five cigarettes, waiting for them to return, watching the face of the Omega, remembering the precise time of sunrise.

For the last twenty minutes he had heard small arms fire from the beach far beyond the trees—the advance raiding party sent to draw off some of the town's defenders.

Frost turned, hearing the scouting party returning from the town, passing the guards Frost had posted outside the staging area. The commander of the scouting party, a Major Davison, an ex-Air Cavalry man, ran over to Frost, started to salute and Frost told him, "Isn't that a little absurd—you're a Major, I'm a Captain and you salute. Tell me what you got."

"Yes, sir. Everything checks out right down to

the scale on the map, sir. The Naval Station looks to have guards on the outside wall—one man for each quadrant, but they've apparently got guards on the ground inside too, now—must have beefed things up after they heard about us yesterday. There looks to be new machine gun emplacements all through the town, rooftops, leading into cellars, things like that—I counted fifteen of them, and like I say, all new looking. Guards around the city, but we saw traffic moving freely enough in and out and it doesn't look like they've mined anything, at least not the roads. Just inside the town there's a big pillbox with three machineguns mounted inside best as we could tell, barbed wire around it. But that's it. Looked to be a lot more activity in and around the base itself and right after the gunfire broke out from the beach, about a hundred men took off out of the Naval Base like bats out of hell toward the beach. I figure that diversionary force suckered 'em good."

"Okay," Frost said. "Anything else?"

"Yeah—they have a tank, one I think. In the middle of the town with a half dozen guards with submachineguns around it."

"Okay," Frost told the man. "Thanks Davison—may as well relax for a couple of minutes. I make it we've got about five minutes or so before we attack. Did a good job."

"Thank you sir," and Davison saluted, holding it until Frost returned, then the man started away. Frost looked at his watch again. It was nearly time. The operation plan was a variant of what he'd used in Genevieve, but the tank added an extra factor. He signalled to Davison, sitting about twenty yards away, Davison coming over again. "Yes, sir?"

"Davison—since you know where that tank is and the rest of your scouting party do too, when we hit, you guys go after it, first thing—use the same infiltration route we mapped out before. If you can get the tank intact, fantastic. Start passing the word around you're looking for somebody who can operate a Soviet built tank. Once you get somebody take him with you and keep him alive until you get it."

"Gotchya, sir," Davison said, starting away.

Frost glanced at his watch—less than two minutes. At any moment now, he should hear the opening salvos as Marina's ships steamed into the harbor under the nose of the Naval Station gun emplacements.

The ground under him seemed to rock then—he made a mental note to definitely investigate the size of the naval gun on Angel One. He glanced at his watch, the explosion still ringing in his ears, the CAR-16 in his hands, his voice shouting as he jumped to his feet, "Let's go!"

And it started again—somebody started it, then someone picked it up. As they passed the first hundred yards in a dead run, gunfire already ringing through the mists around them, it had already become a chant, "Get Ramon! Get Ramon! Get Ramon!"

It was as if the sun had been waiting on a spring—he'd read that in a book someplace—Frost thought, for suddenly it winked above the water visible beyond the Naval Station and the town, almost blinding as Frost and his men raced toward it from all directions. The roar of the naval gun aboard Angel One was not the only roar now, big guns from the Naval Station beginning to respond.

Frost and forty of his men hit the first of the perimeter defenses of the town, machinegun fire pouring down on them, Frost's grenadiers responding, explosions rocking the walls of the town, the machineguns one by one silencing. Then the mortar fire began, from the big pillbox beyond the city entrance Frost judged and he shouted the orders to direct the fire of the grenadiers toward it.

Still running, the machinegun fire dying, they hit the breach in the walls that gave entrance to the town, the pillbox and its three machineguns now opening up, a mortar emplacement somewhere near it shattering the ground around Frost's force, pockmarks and craters appearing everywhere in the aftermath of the impacts, flying bodies and flying limbs crashing down along with the dirt and debris as they ran. Frost's breath froze in his throat—the tank Davison had spoken of was rolling up behind the pillbox. Frost shouted to his men to fall off and take up flanking positions on both sides of the opening in the walls, shouting to the grenadiers to keep pouring it on the pillbox.

Frost saw Corporal Carr, a LAWS rocket going to his shoulder, the tank opening fire with its turret gun, but rather than its massive shell impacting against Frost and his mercenaries, the shell blasted away the top of the pillbox, the machineguns, part of the mortar emplacement and the bodies of the men who had manned the weapons hurtled skyward. Frost shouted to Carr, "Can that LAWS, kid—Davison got the damned tank!"

Rallying his men, Frost started forward again, changing sticks on the CAR-16, like the rest of his men firing at targets of opportunity. The tank was visible ahead, moving up on the pillbox, firing into it again, dirt and flame and debris mushrooming upward as the shell hit. Then the turret began to wheel, the gun firing, a section of the wall on Frost's right collapsing, the Communist defenders on it falling and silenced. Frost stopped running, letting his men pass him, bringing Carr and three others with him, half jogging, half walking toward the tank. Davison stuck his head up through the lid on the tank, a big grin across his face shouting, "We do good boss?"

"Ya did good," Frost smiled, lighting a cigarette, letting the fighting move ahead of him. "Let's get that tank of yours moving ahead of us, pass up our boys and see if we can beat everybody to the Naval Station walls—that thing's gonna come in handy there."

"Gotchya, sir," Davison shouted back. The tank wheeled around the crater that had been the pillbox and Frost and the few of his men he'd taken along with Corporal Carr hung after it, returning fire at occasional shooters from rooftops or windows or doorways as the tank rumbled ahead of them. The ground still rocked from the concussion of the naval gun aboard Angel One, the answering fire from the Naval Station coming more quickly now as the tank reached the midpoint in the city. Frost and Carr and some of the others clambered up on the tank, Frost banging on the lid, Davison opening it, "Yo!"

"Let's boogey, Major—we got our seatbelts," Frost shouted.

"Gotchya, sir," Davison shouted back, turning his face away into the bowels of the tank, "Get her goin.' Harlan!"

The tank lurched ahead then, the big gun booming occasionally into the side of a building from where heavy small arms fire was emanating. And always the small arms fire stopped. Frost smiled—the tank was a stroke of good luck he hadn't counted on.

The outside walls of the Naval Station were visible ahead, heavy fighting on and near the walls and Frost ordered Davison, the lid still open on the tank, "Start firing into that wall—faster we get to those gun emplacements faster Timmons can launch his men."

"Right!" Davison shouted back over the din of gunfire.

The tank settled in edging forward a few more yards then stopping. Frost rasped to the men around him, "Hold your ears and get down," then himself jumped to the ground behind the tank, taking cover. The gun boomed, Frost looked beyond the tank body and saw a four foot

130

hole in the adobe wall, more of the wall cracked and starting to crumble. He barely got his hands to his ears as the massive Russian gun fired again, the rest of the facing portion of the outside wall crumbling, then the tank starting to rumble forward. There was one more machinegun nest, just outside the walls and to their right, the gun still chattering, the tank driver apparently not noticing it. Frost snatched the LAWS rocket from the hands of Corporal Carr, slung away his rifle and shouldered the green rocket tube, checking the sights, checking that he was clear behind, then pulling the trigger, the rocket gushing from the tube, its smoke trail visible as it streaked toward the machinegun nest, the guns, the men—everything in the hollow by the far building wall—going up as the rocket exploded. Frost tossed the tube away, rasping, "Not nice to litter," then with Carr and the others followed along behind the tank, the big gun just firing, a shell impacting on the wall to their left, taking a half moon shaped chunk out of the top of the wall, the roof of a building barely visible behind it exploding as well. The tank rumbled over the debris, Frost and the others climbing over it, the second, better defended wall looming up ahead of them. Someone was running up with a rocket launcher and Frost directed Carr and the others, along with himself, to start firing toward the man—the last thing he needed now was to lose the tank. The tank kept going, stopping a hundred yards from the second wall, then starting once again to fire.

The tank moved ahead, a healthy chunk blown out of the seaward side of the wall ahead of them, Frost signalling his commanders to rally the men for the last assault against the gun emplacements. Leaving the comparative shelter of the tank, Frost and as many as a hundred of his men started through the huge chink in the defensive wall and across the parade ground area beyond, the Soviet- and Cuban-taught Monte Azulian defenders streaming from buildings and defensive positions and meeting Frost and his men hand to hand, gunfire, screams, the whoosh and roar of the M-79 grenade launchers, all of it mingling with the firing of the naval gun and the shore based guns from the Naval Station.

Frost would move forward a yard or so, there was a target of opportunity. He would fire, one, perhaps two of the Communist defenders would run forward, Frost taking them on with his bayonet if necessary, the blade dripping with glistening blood before he had gone fifty yards through the slaughterhouse around him.

Beyond a low wall, Frost could see the shore guns themselves, belching fire and smoke as they streamed their rounds down into the harbor, and onto Angels One and Three and the invasion force. Frost shouted to some of his commanders, "Form on me—we're going after the guns!" He estimated there were perhaps fifty men already with him when he shouted, "Now!" Frost began to run, forward, his CAR-16 streaming lead as he pushed ahead, the men around him in a wedge, the roar of small arms fire around him like an ex-

132

plosion in an ammunition factory, wave upon wave of the Communist defenders starting to counter attack, then falling back toward the guns. They reached the platform like rocks at the far end of the Naval Station on which the guns were set, but only at the far end. The harbor was visible. Frost could see small boats moving across the glassy surface, see shells from the shore based guns exploding around Angels One and Three, see the fire and smoke as the deck gun on Angel One returned fire. Frost glanced from side to side, counting roughly forty men, then getting up from his crouch, a fresh magazine loaded in the rifle he started forward, leading his men against the gun emplacement. As Frost moved ahead, he shifted the CAR fully to his right hand, snatching the KG-9 on its makeshift sling into his left hand, awkwardly one-handed getting the bolt cocked and then starting to fire the semi-automatic 9mm pistol as well, the CAR still firing from his right hand.

The Communists had massed for a final counter attack, Frost realized, the first wave starting toward them across the flat surface rocks in a rush, bayonets bristling on their Communist origin rifles, the rifles themselves firing full automatic and cutting into Frost's attacking force. Below in the harbor as Frost glanced down he could see the first elements of Timmons' landing forces coming ashore but there was a good quarter mile or more for Timmons' forces to fight their way over before reaching Frost and his men at the fortresses.

Frost kept moving, firing his guns until they were empty, reloading, closing the distance with the enemy—all of it in seconds.

He couldn't see Carr—had the kid bought it? Frost asked himself. Nice kid . . .

"Captain Frost!"

Frost turned, slowing, and then he saw Carr, the young corporal having rallied perhaps two dozen of Frost's men, coming up from Frost's right, flanking the counterattacking Communist force. Frost shouted to his own men, "Come on!" and he started to run.

They closed with the Communist force then, Frost's rifle and the KG-9 shot out and no time to reload, Frost's bayonet working like a rapier, the Metalified Browning High Power shoved in his belt coming into his left hand to fire a two round burst, then stuffed away as Frost fought his way ahead with the bayonet fixed to the muzzle of his assault rifle.

Face after face, thrust after thrust, blood spattering on his hands and clothes, the shouts and screams of agony and the sporadic small arms fire around him blending together. The Communist counter-offensive was beginning to crumble as Frost and his men linked with Carr's men, then Frost and Carr together with a surviving thirty men who could walk or run charged toward the guns, Frost reaching the last defensive wall, firing his CAR-16 again, his men streaming over the wall behind him. As the last of the Communists began to lay down their arms, Frost, leaning against a wall, collared Carr as the young Corporal passed him. "Hey," Frost shouted, trying to catch his breath.

"Yes, sir?"

"For what it's worth, I'm giving you a field commission to Second Lieutenant—I mean, there won't be an army for you to hold the commission with if we win, and if we lose once we hit Monte Azul, we'll be dead—but don't get it in your blood, kid," and Frost pushed away from the wall and started toward the gun emplacements where some of his commanders were already assembling. He turned and shouted back to the boy, "Well . . . come on!"

An hour later, Frost's face dirty, his camouflage fatigues blood spattered, the muzzles of his guns stained black from powder residue, he stood beside Marina Aguillara-Garcia as she raised the flag of Monte Azul over the town and Naval Base of Normandie—her comparatively tiny feet stood on the black and purple banner of the Communists. The cry went up, from the soldiers, the people of the town—even Frost himself, he thought: "Get Ramon! Liberation!"

Chapter Fourteen

Frost stood on the beach, the water lapping up close to his black combat booted feet, something like a burrito in his left hand—he was starving. He finished the last of the burrito or whatever it was—he hadn't asked when the townspeople had brought the food—and watched as the rubber boats left filled with men and returned empty, the launches salvaged from the Naval Station doing the same. Frost lit a cigarette and pulled the bottle of Cerveza from his hip pocket, twisted on the cap—it didn't twist—and wished for a moment he had an Israeli Galil—they were the only assault rifles he could think of at the moment that came standard with a bottle opener and wire cutter attachment. Frost walked back toward the seawall and found a likely looking rock and pried the cap off the tepid beer bottle and cocked the bottle mouth back against his, almost choking on the warm liquid but drinking it anyway. He leaned against the seawall and lit a Camel in the blue yellow flame of the battered Zippo he carried, dropping the Zippo back in his pocket. Marina was coming down the beach and he figured she could see him. He was too tired to walk over to her—she could come to him, he thought.

Marina, in her blue jeans and a blue T-shirt, kept walking, toward him, a scarf in her left hand—presumably the one that had been tied over her hair earlier when they'd raised the flag over the Naval Station. There was a web pistol belt slung low on her hips, a holster swinging from it, the flap open and the butt of one of the Smith & Wesson revolvers from the ship's stores visible there. It was an odd costume he thought—she wore sandals and no stockings. She stopped, a yard or so from him, smiling, saying, "We have come far—General."

"I have come farther, kid," Frost smiled back. "I got the bruises to prove it."

"And now?"

"And now, back to the boats as we're do-ing—before Ramon comes to get us. I'm leaving enough people to hold the town against anything except a mass assault and they can man the har-bor guns, too. I think Angel Two—she's pretty empty—can . . . I mean, Angel Three—got my angels mixed up. Angel Three, anyway," Frost continued, "can get close enough in to the docks that we can crane over that Soviet tank—might prove useful once we hit Monte Azul."

"When, Hank?"

Frost looked at the girl thinking somehow she was more interested in winning her war than in him. "Dawn—day after tomorrow—Ramon's guys seem to be late risers—worked for us in the past. We can use those gunboats to get our men onto the beaches, then for fire support."

"Esta bien," she smiled.

"You can say that again," Frost cracked, finishing the beer.

Chapter Fifteen

In all, Frost figured, standing against the bow rail of Angel One, they had netted twelve more gunboats, and with the three from the smaller naval base and the three salvaged and still afloat from the encounter on the high seas, that made eighteen. There was one small missile cruiser—at least Blackie Torres had called it small. It had looked big to him, Frost thought. And, there were one or two inboard pleasure boats apparently having belonged to some of Ramon's officers stationed at Normandie. Frost had placed Davison in charge of having them fitted with heavy machineguns so they would be useful in the assault. In both battles on the island of Sabot, Frost had lost a total of sixty-eight dead, fifty-seven injured, and of those injured at least thirty of them were such minor injuries the men would be back on duty within twenty-four hours. The man who'd been bitten in the swamp had lost his fever and been given Tetanus boosters and put on a course of antibiotics—he was vastly improved.

Frost thought of Carr, the young man now an "officer" and a seasoned fighter. "It goes on for forever," Frost heard himself mutter as he lit a cigarette.

Frost had slept part of that afternoon and it was coming on now toward darkness. He checked the Omega on his wrist. In two hours, he was due to leave the main body of what he decided now could rightly be called a "fleet" and with a band of eleven volunteers—Timmons included—he would get as close as possible offshore at their landing site, then using scuba gear they would go inland to reconnoiter the beach defense. Because of Monte Azul's geography there were only three possible attack zones and Frost knew that and knew that Ramon knew it as well—and Frost assumed one would be as good as another. Part of what he had jokingly called his "master plan" was another diversion using Angel Three and a half dozen gunboats at the spot furthest down the coast. Hopefully, Frost planned to draw off some of Ramon's reserve forces—the beach assault was going to be costly enough he knew and every life he might save through a diversion was worth it. Once the attack actually began, Angel Three would move off to

140

the third spot in the middle of the three possible landing sites, and Frost knew this too might delude Ramon, confusing him as to which was the actual attack and which was the diversion.

Frost pushed himself away from the bow rail and started below, seeing Timmons and collaring the man, "Hey—how's the equipment looking for tonight?" Frost asked, pausing in what Frost had learned was called a companionway instead of a hall or corridor.

"Bloody well, sir," Timmons returned, back stiff as a ramrod.

"Relax, man," Frost told him, the Britisher standing easy then.

"I had twice as many volunteers as we needed, sir, so I was able to pick and choose a bit—got a good crew of lads we have."

"Fine, Timmons," Frost said, then started into his cabin. He needed to be alone—the constant press of people, the questions for orders, the details—they were driving him insane, he thought. He took the Browning from his hip, tossing the leather belt holster and webbed belt on the bunk. He unfolded a rag and took out the Break-Free CLP lubricant, the Browning's cleaning rod—he used one of the old-style metal rods from a Walther PPK/S—they were plastic these days, and probably better he thought. He dumped the magazine in the Browning, then jacked back the slide, clearing the chambered round and remagazining it. He locked the slide back, then removed the slide stop, then unlocked the slide and let it travel forward, inverting it and

141

moving out the recoil spring and the barrel, then beginning to clean. He thought about Bess —there was no way to contact her, to find how the operation to remove the rest of the bullet fragments had gone. They were binding against a nerve in her right hip, preventing her use of the right leg—crippling her. Each time Frost thought of the terrorist attack on them, he boiled inside. He had gotten both the man and the woman, but they had wounded him, not seriously, and crippled Bess. After that, it had been bad—once she was well, he didn't know exactly how it would be. She wanted him to quit. If this thing with Marina worked out, he knew, he'd be able to—one hundred thousand dollars. But would he. As he planned it now, he thought, after Monte Azul had been retaken—if it could be retaken—there was a cabin a friend of his had up in the mountains between Albuquerque and Santa Fe. He could stay there a few days, a few weeks, maybe get his life in order.

There was a knocking at the cabin door and Frost rasped, "Come on in!"

He turned, looking over his shoulder —Marina.

"Hi kid," he smiled, then turned back to cleaning his gun.

"Frost?"

"Yeah," he answered.

"Yo pienso—I think tonight that you do not have to go, not on the mission to the beach—you should—"

"What? Just 'cause you're calling me a general doesn't mean I can sit back all nice and safe and let everybody else take the chances—I'm not that way, kid. Anyway, I want to check out those beach defenses myself—then I can really tell what's going on and what kind of chances we've got.''

"What kind of chances do we have?'' She asked, sitting down beside him, her left hand on his right thigh.

"Well,'' and Frost finished wiping down the gun, then began reassembly—the barrel went back into the slide first.

"Well?''

"I guess we have a pretty good chance,'' he told her. "Unless we get stalled too long on the beach. Now, last you told me, Commacho's nephew is still supposed to meet us, fight his way through as soon as we begin our attack, to divert some of Ramon's forces and link up with us. Fine, if it all works, terrific. But, if we sit on that beach too long, we're out of business—Ramon's Cuban air support can knock hell out of us. We have to hit fast, get into fortified positions, hope those machineguns and the smaller naval guns we heisted off Sabot will work effectively as anti-aircraft pieces, then just hold on until Commacho's people get with us.''

"And what if anything of this goes wrong, even a small thing?''

"Well, depends on what small thing,'' Frost told her, wiping his hands on the rag and getting up to wash them in the small bathroom—he guessed you called a bathroom a bathroom. "If

143

it's something really small, we can work around it. You mean though, say, Commacho's troops don't make it through, something like that? Well, then we get back on our little boats and we try to float away and hope nobody notices us and you are out a country and I'm out my money."

"And what if we win, Hank?"

"Then it's peaches and cream for everybody, kid," Frost smiled, coming back from the small sink, drying his hands on the sides of his pants —he couldn't find a towel.

"I mean—if I am Presidenta, I will need to hold my country, I will need—I will need you."

"Look," Frost smiled, sitting down beside her, putting his right arm across her shoulders. "Probably a lot of the guys will stay on if you ask them to—a lot of them, at least for a while. You'll do all right."

"What about you, Hank?" she asked, her dark eyes seeming to bore into him.

"I'll hang on until you settle in, but that won't be more than a week or two after we get things secure—then—"

"No," the girl said, emphatically.

"Yes," he told her, still smiling.

"As Presidenta, I will need someone, someone strong to lead my army, to organize my police—I will need, somebody," she repeated.

"You'll find somebody—there are lots of competent people—I can help you find them."

"I will need you," she told him.

"Look—we talked about it. I never told you," and he started to bring up Bess, but didn't. "I

144

never told you, but I can't—see, if I stayed, everything else in my own life aside, what would I be? Huh? Your crown prince or something? No thanks—I don't—"

"You can be what you want, to me, to Monte Azul. You feel for the people for our fight—it is not the money that makes you fight as you do."

"Yeah," Frost said. "I feel for them, and I hate Ramon's thing as much as you do, and I want to fight the Communists, and I fight—I believe. But I'm still me," Frost told her.

"Si, pero—but you can still be yourself—but make being with me a part of this, no?"

"No," Frost told her. "You are beautiful. I enjoy loving with you—I think we have something between us, but I can't live with you being the leader of a country—what the hell kind of life would we have—never alone, always worrying about the crackpots—" Frost stopped, lit a cigarette and stared at his reflection in the porthole glass—he realized he was throwing the same thing at her basically that Bess always threw at him. He looked at Marina. "When I get back after tonight—let's talk more then?"

"Si," she smiled, but her eyes not smiling.

Frost watched as she walked out of the cabin, closing the door behind herself. He reloaded his gun, sitting on the edge of the bunk saying, "Oh, my God," shaking his head—"Where am I going?"

Chapter Sixteen

Frost, Timmons and the ten other men had packed aboard the largest of the converted pleasure boats, the boat low in the water as it had left the main body of the fleet and headed toward the dark and distant outline of the Monte Azulian shoreline.

This time, Frost wore a full wet suit as did the others, black hood and all, the oxygen tanks the best Communist Cuba could provide Ernesto Ramon's forces as were the suits. Brand new, never-used diving knives were strapped to Frost's right leg and the right legs of the other men, the men's individual weapons in plastic under their wet suits. The Greaseguns used in the earlier sea foray had been cleaned and some of these were now on hand along with one M-16 fitted with a standard Colt commercial scope, this in a plastic waterproof case.

The rumbling of the launch's motors stopped and Frost waited for the quiet, listening. He could see little still of the shoreline, though it was much closer than it had been when they'd left the fleet. Frost cleaned off the interior of his mask, leaned down and sloshed it in the small waves lapping against the side of the boat, then put it on, pulling it down in place and finding the mouthpiece attachment for the diving lung.

"Everybody over the side, stick with me, always keep two men in sight—no lights unless you get attacked by something—" there were sharks in the waters off the coast of Monte Azul, Frost knew, "and no noise. If you do get attacked unless it's life or death, just stick with your knives, or get some one of us with a speargun to come in—don't use a firearm unless you have to. They don't work too hot under water anyway and they don't keep working very well at all. Questions."

Frost expected some comment from Timmons, but there was none, the bearded, blue-eyed bull of an Englishman as silent as a tomb—wrong word, Frost thought. Tomb was definitely the wrong thing to think about tonight, he told himself.

"No questions," Frost said, putting the mouthpiece up and rolling over the side and into the dark waters. He started swimming off, the others following him in, the water almost cold seeming compared to the daylight air temperature and even the air temperature of the night.

Frost counted to himself as the others entered the water and when the eleventh man—Timmons, obvious by his bulk—hit, Frost started off through the water, toward the coastline. They didn't dare take the risk of using a light, he knew —an air patrol that might be sweeping overhead could spot the glow underwater for possibly miles—the night was clear. The converted pleasure boat that had brought them would pull farther off shore and wait, coming in once and that —Frost checked his watch, the luminous dial clear in the murky blackness—would be in precisely five hours. Pacing himself, he kept going, the only sound that of his air tanks. He slowed, backstroking a moment as a school of some small, and to Frost unrecognizable fish passed in front of him, then started on again.

The swim took thirty minutes even as Frost stuck his head up out of the surf, then seeing nothing tucked back down, signalling the others, then started in toward the shore. He'd stripped away the waterproof covering on the Greasegun already and stowed it, not caring if the gun got wet—he'd need it for but a few hours. He'd seen discarded guns in Viet Nam—and sometimes they had been booby trapped. It was universal the way it was known that Americans liked war trophies and a few men Frost had known had died in their pursuit. He thought back to his father—he remembered that there had been a Luger with all matching serials, even on the magazine. There had been a 7.65mm Walther PPK with Wermacht grips. But to a degree, Frost thought, the wars of the earlier part of the century had been between men who had at least a veneer of civilization—there had not been children with plastique strapped to their chests then.

Frost hit the beach in a low crouch, the Greasegun's stubby muzzle moving across the sand like a wand—a death wand, not a magical one.

Frost glanced behind him. Fanned out along the beach, hugging to whatever protection there was were the other eleven men. Frost started forward in a fast, dead run. Reaching a pile of rocks at the far side of the beach he stopped, on his knees beside them, listening, hearing his heart beating wildly in his chest, his breathing—but no sign of Ramon's men. Timmons was beside him a moment later, the big bearded Britisher red-faced in the moonlight. Frost signalled for Timmons to follow him, then started into the rocks. The other ten men all had their assigned tasks, sweeping up and down the length of the beach, two of them going back into the water to search as best they could in darkness for nets, pits, anything that might prove a deadfall on the actual invasion beach a quarter mile south. With Timmons behind him now, Frost moved higher into the rocks. The clanging of his equipment sounded like noise from a boiler factory as he moved, Frost thought, though he knew it was virtually nothing. Unlike the movies, he hadn't thrown away his mask or flippers—he would

149

need them for the swim back if he made it.

Frost stopped, Timmons bumping up behind him. He'd heard something and now, the Metalified Browning High Power in his right fist as he edged forward, Frost stopped again—voices, speaking in Spanish. Dropping to his knees and elbows, Frost edged along the rocks, listening. He could hear the voices plainly now—men, laughing, joking, but the Spanish was too fast for him to make anything out beyond a few words here and there.

Frost reached into the waterproof air-padded musette bag slung diagonally across his chest and extracted a small tape recorder—one of the men aboard the Angel Three used it to send talking letters home when he could. Frost punched the record button, the volume up as high as possible, then punched for play. He set the recorder down, left Timmons to watch it and keep tabs on the soldiers, then started off again further into the rocks, signalling Timmons by hand that he would be back soon.

The rocks started sloping downward and Frost followed them, stopping again when he heard voices—this time he could understand the Spanish—two men, speaking softly, discussing a woman. And beyond them, Frost spotted what he had feared most. Just how it had gotten through the jungle to here he was uncertain—another of the Soviet tanks. He stared at it a moment, thinking. His right hand smoothed at his mustache, then the salt and pepper stubbled smile-frown lines in his face creased into a grin.

He knew now what he would have to do immediately prior to the invasion.

Frost edged back up the sloping rocks and back toward Timmons. He sat in the rocks for another ten minutes, recording the conversation that had switched to a more serious subject—it was a group of officers from the coastal defense, and they were discussing just that for a time As the officers moved off, so did Frost and Timmons, Frost leading the big man back in the direction of the tank, but farther up into the rocks, so close Frost could smell the jungle, but giving the tank a wide berth. As they moved, stopping periodically, Frost gradually counted six tanks—Ramon quite definitely expected an invasion. There were mortar emplacements, dugout machinegun nests and further up a long trench that would likely accommodate fifty men and provided firing steps for them.

Frost made another mental note on his invisible invasion plan, the thought amusing him.

The time allowed for the reconnaissance ashore passed quickly and Frost and Timmons' rendezvous with the other ten men in the surf—forty minutes remained before the ship would be in position to pick them up. As Frost pulled the mask in place, checked the waterproof closure on the air padded musette bag with the tape recorder and the precious—he hoped—recording, he thought about two things: tanks and trenches. His invasion might be a little easier—and bloodier—than he'd planned.

Chapter Seventeen

The yellow light swayed over the galley table—
there was a storm blowing that had started brew-
ing as Frost and the other eleven men had
returned to the Angel One. There had been a
debriefing session, the tape had been evaluated
by Marina and Blackie Torres, Captain of Angel
One, the two the most literate of Spanish speak-
ers available. And now, sheafs of reports available, translated notes from the tapes on the
table, Frost, Timmons, Davison, Carr—Frost
liked the boy—and Marina sat with Blackie
Torres, drinking coffee and rum and sifting
through the reports. It was four in the morning
and the decision had to be made soon, Frost
determined, whether to go the next morning or

not—perhaps within a half hour if he wanted a dawn attack.

Frost sipped at his coffee, having given up on the Myers Rum despite its goodness.

"Damn," he muttered. "You read this?" and he looked at Marina. Then he smiled—she and Torres, he remembered, had translated it. Too much rum, he decided.

"Si—they know our strength, they expect us, they are waiting—those tanks. Madre de Dios!"

"Ohhh," Frost sighed, dragging heavily on the Camel between his fingers. "Well, I know what I do now, just not when—that's the damned pain of the whole thing! When?"

"What will you do," Blackie Torres asked.

"Very simple," Frost smiled, the yellow light casting weird shadows on his hands and—he imagined—on his face as it swayed overhead. "I go in with a commando force before first light, we snitch the tanks, I fill the trench there with gasoline, then when Ramon's troops head into it, I light it—simple. Just not enough time, not for training, not for getting into position—nothing. I've decided," Frost said. "Not tomorrow, but the day after. I know that gives them more time to prepare, but by the same token they're going to wonder what we're up to. So—any reasons why we shouldn't wait?"

Frost looked around the table. "Good—then I'll have some more rum—since I'm not working early."

After the meeting broke up, Frost having ordered a day off the next day for everyone who was a nonessential person, Frost sat under yellow light, alone except for Marina, listening to the quiet.

"What are you thinking," the girl asked him.

"Oh, about you, about a girl named Bess—I think I mentioned her once to you, about everything, about nothing. If I knew what I were thinking, I wouldn't be busy thinking about it, would I?"

"What kind of person are you?"

"Me—best definition I could ever come up with," he said, drinking some of the rum, then sipping at his coffee.

"Do you want to get drunk, fall into bed with me and make love?"

"All but the drunk part—you know, in my exalted position," and Frost drank some of the rum again.

"The make love part—it's okay, you like?"

"Yeah—it is okay, I like."

"Do you know how to say I love you in Spanish, Hank?"

"Sure," Frost laughed. "I love you in Spanish. Simple, huh?"

"No—the words—yo te amo, see?"

"Was that see like look or si like yes?"

"I love you," the girl told him, dropping on her knees beside his chair. Frost set the glass of rum down, dragged heavily at the coffee cup and looked at her.

"Thank you," he whispered.

"Si—like yes," she laughed.

"Si—I love you now—I don't know how

much, how long—but now," and Frost bent down and kissed her cheek.

"Now?"

"Si," Frost told her, "like yes—si, now," and Frost bent to her, his arms folding around her as he pulled her onto his lap.

"I love you," she repeated.

Frost kissed her, half to shut her up—he always seemed to be doing that he thought—and half because he wanted to. He kissed her again—all because he wanted to.

"Hank?"

"Si," he whispered.

"I am glad you do not go tomorrow—we shall make love the rest of tonight, then tomorrow—I need you."

"Yes," Frost smiled, sounding terribly sober to himself but not quite feeling that way at all. "But who do you need—Hank Frost the passionate lover, or Hank Frost the counterfeit generalissimo of the Army and admiral of the Navy, the intrepid freedom fighter, the guy who runs around and plays army for money? Who do you need, kid?"

"I need you, carino."

"Yeah," Frost almost snarled. "What's Spanish for 'blood of my veins' or something?"

"Yo no entiende, carino."

"Yo pienso," Frost began, realizing his grammar wasn't up to it, "tu quierra me por," and then it failed him completely and he rasped, "Hell—I think you want me for a soldier, kid—not for me. You maybe think you want me for

155

me, but it's just the uniform . . . like they say in the movies."

"You drink too much."

"I used to drink a lot more," Frost said.

"You do not think I love you?"

"Oh, yeah—you do, but which me is it you love, kid?"

"The whole you, everything, all of the things about you, Hank."

"Sounds like a song cue," Frost murmured. "Well—here we are anyway. I'm not much good at making love on chairs anyway—let's head to the cabin, hmmm?"

"Si, carino."

"Si, si—this is a funny thing, kid," Frost told her.

"Why?"

"Our lines got switched in the translation." Then standing, Frost took the girl's hands in his and kissed her, the yellow light swaying above them, casting them periodically into light and shadow. His right arm going around her, any trace of the rum gone from him now, he started with her out of the galley and down the long companionway toward the cabin. They went inside, Frost fumbling the light on. He dropped the pistol belt on the chair beside the bed, then took the girl in his arms again, crushing her mouth under his as he kissed her, almost savagely. There was something about the prospect of death, Frost realized, that made life more intense, the smallest thing or the grandest thing that much sweeter or more poignant. He held her hands lightly a moment, held them as she undid the buttons on the shirt she wore. Then suddenly it was gone and her hands went behind her a moment to undo the white bra she wore, this slipping forward from her shoulders, one of the straps still hooked on her wrist as she folded her arms around his neck.

Frost's hands explored her, then he kissed her shoulders, feeling her fumble past him for the lightswitch, then there was darkness except for the moonlight streaming through the cabin porthole. They sat together on the bunk for a few moments, the girl holding his hands against her, then leaned back across the bunk. "I do not want this to end," she whispered. Frost slipping his eyepatch and his wrist watch on the the small nightstand beside them, knew that it would.

Chapter Eighteen

There was one overflight the following afternoon by an unmarked Soviet jet fighter and
likely, Frost surmised, flown by a Cuban pilot.
As the plane crossed low over the Angel One,
evident it wasn't opening fire, Frost started waving to it, soon joined by the other mercenaries
and ship's crew on deck at the time. The late
afternoon was spent in preparation for the commando raid that would precede the main invasion at dawn the following morning, Frost and
the same eleven men, including Timmons, plus
six other men—these not brought along because
of particular skill with demolitions, in
clandestine operations, etc. They knew, instead,
how to handle a tank. In addition to these, Frost

brought Major Davison in on the operation, to co-ordinate the tank force once it was captured and turned against the beach defenders— Davison would later be officially in charge of the beachhead defenses once they were established, Frost seeing the providential tanks as an integral part of these.

As night came, Frost tried to mentally prepare for the battle that was to come, forcing himself to try to relax. After a light dinner and a glass of rum, he stood in the darkness near the bow rail, smoking. The Browning High Power, the hybrid CAR-16, the KG-9—they were all cleaned, checked, each spare magazine carefully loaded. The two Gerber knives, the M-16 bayonet—these too were cleaned, sharpened and lightly oiled. The scuba gear, the demolitions equipment, the jellied gasoline, all of it was ready. There was an ancillary advantage to the commando raid, Frost knew—it might further put off suspicion that this was the site of the actual invasion attempt. The overflight by the Communist jet fighter worried him, in that there had been no gunplay. How many more of the jet fighters there were available, Frost couldn't guess. Heavy air supports for Ramon's government troops would spell a defeat, and Frost knew that—the one thing he sorely lacked was air support. He shrugged and tried to put the thoughts out of his mind—this business of being a general, he thought, was something to which he had no intention of becoming accustomed. "Learn by doing," he murmured. There was a friend he had, and the man

159

had always kiddingly said the words "Learn by doing" were his family motto. Frost laughed, deciding it should be his as well.

He stared out across the water, then down to the Omega on his wrist—he could get to like the sea, he decided. Maybe, after he got paid, he'd drop a thousand or so and take one of those rough-it cruises in the Carribean for a week or ten days—it would be nice to do that with Bess he thought, wondering suddenly how the operation had gone.

He shook his head to clear it, checking the wrist watch again, deciding to get an hour's or so worth of extra sleep . . .

He had slept, soundly, too soundly and now, sitting in the small lean-to like cabin of one of the converted pleasure boats, the cabin serving as the wheelhouse, Frost wished that he hadn't. He lit a Camel, then thought better of it—the napalm was too near. Carefully, he flipped the cigarette over the side, then stood on the starboard rail watching the dark shape of the Monte Azul coastline looming up ahead of them—the boat would return to the fleet to fulfill its role in the invasion—a one-way trip this time.

Frost reminded himself what he was doing—fighting Communism, fighting the ignorance and dehumanization and terror it spawned. He decided to feel noble, a crusader, a hero perhaps—if not quite from the standard heroic mold. He pulled up the hood on the wetsuit as the engines stopped and the craft drifted for a few moments. He slipped the oxygen tank onto

160

his shoulders, tightening the fastenings around his waist, pulling on the fins. The old .45 Greasegun was getting another workout tonight—already the thing was starting to pit from two exposures to saltwater. His personal weapons secure in a pack attached to an oxygen tank-shaped aquascooter, they lowered this over the side, Frost sitting backwards on the railing, bringing up his mouthpiece and lowering his mask. He rolled back, Timmons next, then Davison, then one by one the others, Frost already starting the scooter, Timmons, Davison and the others starting the scooters they had, seven of them in all, the men holding to each other by the shoulder or leg, letting the scooters pull them along. Tonight, no one could afford to be tired by a long swim— and the converted pleasure boat had stopped two miles further off shore.

There was a light attachment on the scooter, but Frost didn't use it, neither did any of the others as they moved quickly and silently through the dark waters. In the distance, Frost thought he made out the outline of a shark fin and he clutched at the spear gun attached to the aquascooter, but then the outline disappeared.

After what Frost considered surprisingly little time—he had never used one of the aquascooters before—they reached the surf, leaving the scooters behind as they started up through the waves and across the sand, Frost snapping off the mask and hooking it over his elbow, the Greasegun unlimbered from its plastic covering, taking a bath as a wave crashed over Frost as he raced in a low crouch along the still slightly moonlit beach, then up and toward the rocks.

The men gathered around him now, Frost, with hand and arm signals, directed them to begin—each had assigned tasks of sabotage or assault. Frost, Timmons, Davison and the six tank operators started for the first of the tanks while others started toward the massive defensive trench to fill it with the napalm.

Frost started climbing higher into the rocks, then down, toward where he had seen the first tank the previous evening and early morning. It was still there, some of Ramon's troops casually lounging around it. The rest of the weapons already unlimbered, the scuba gear except for the wetsuits stashed in the rocks, Frost started forward, the CAR-16, the KG-9 and the Greasegun slung to his body, but in his right hand the long bladed knife. Timmons and Davison and the others following his lead, Frost edged as closely as possible to the nearest of the Ramon troopers, then clearing his mind, focusing his attention on the man's body falling as the knife struck, Frost pushed himself up, racing forward, jumping on the man's back, the big knife driving into the throat to rip out the voice box before there could be a cry or scream, then Frost dragging the man down into the sand, jabbing the knife into the right kidney and letting the body slump away. He could see in the gathering darkness before the dawn that Timmons and the others had taken their men as well—there had been no screams yet and there was no alert. Davison was already directing the men who had operated the tank in Normandie to clamber aboard, the plan to be ready to move but not start the tank until at least three more were secured. With Timmons, Davison and the other tank operators, Frost, his knife blade red tinged in what light there was, edged forward toward the location of the second tank, further up the beach.

The second tank was more formally guarded, but with fewer men—four totally, forming a ragged square on each corner of the vehicle. Frost took the man on the left, as he drove the knife in smashing the man's skull against the tank body itself. Davison posted another tank driver and Frost and Timmons and Davison then moved on, four of the would-be tank drivers with them.

The third tank was heavily guarded only because it was nearer what Frost determined as the main camp of the Ramon coastal forces. There was no safe approach with knives, so Frost, Timmons and the others formed up in a tight wedge and charged into the clear space, their Greaseguns roaring, cutting down the guards surrounding the tank, one of Frost's bursts cutting down a man on the tank turret as he tried to clamber inside.

Davison posted a man to the tank and already, Frost could hear the other two captured tanks warming up—it had been arranged that at the first sound of gunfire, the tank drivers should get their machines into action. Frost and Davison and Timmons broke off from the perimeter of

163

the camp, heavy small arms fire already starting to pour toward them. Frost knew that he must get at least one more tank, and with his crew he raced over the rocks toward where he had located the fourth tank. Reaching a high point in the blackish rocks, Frost stopped—the tank was already moving. Frost reached to his web belt, snatching at a grenade, shouting to Timmons, "I'll take it—like we planned. Be ready," and Frost raced out and down the rocks and across the sand, toward the tank, its lid still opened, the turret turning toward him. Jumping and swinging up his hands, he grasped the turret gun's barrel, then his legs swung out and he clambered onto the turret itself, hurtling the grenade into the open tank. There were shouts, curses and as Frost jumped to the sand, going into a roll, the tank crew started out from the hatch, Frost firing the Greasegun at almost point blank range as the driverless tank rolled past him on its massive treads. Frost's subgun fire caught two of the three man crew, a third going down as he raced—simultaneously—toward the rocks where Timmons and Davison were. "Come on!" Frost shouted, then, "That was only a dummy—I made the grenade inert this afternoon!"

The tank driver Davison had selected was already running toward the tank, pushing himself up on it and starting to clamber inside. "Four," Frost smiled, then started back into the shelter of the rocks, enemy small arms fire starting to find him, bullets chewing into the sand as he ran.

Frost reached the rocks, then with Davison

and Timmons and the last two tank drivers started after the remaining Ramon Soviet-built tanks, Frost watching across the rocks as the four already taken tanks linked up and started a drive toward the camp, their turret guns booming.

The next tank was already rolling and buttoned up as well—the inert grenade gag wouldn't work again, Frost thought. And, the new Soviet tanks were so well armored, even a LAWS rocket was no certainty against one. Davison and Timmons each had M-79s with them and Frost, watching the tank rolling toward them, its turret twisting side to side as it searched out a target, shouted over the roar of gunfire, "Start digging holes with those M-79s—get the tank to dip down into one—hurry," and then Frost snatched one of the LAWS rockets from one of the two remaining tank drivers, reasoning, "Looks like your job is getting phased out, fella," and running forward, Frost readied the LAWS, dropping down behind the marginal protection of a low outcropping of rocks, the M-79s already whooshing their grenades ahead of the tank, cratering the sand, the tank twisting its turret toward Davison, Timmons and the other two of Frost's men as it rolled down into the crater formed by the grenade, then started rolling up. As it started out of the trench, the nose of the tank aimed diagonally upward, Frost fired, the LAWS making its loud whoosh and its trail of white smoke as it sped toward the tank's softly armored underbelly, Frost tucking down behind the rocks to protect himself. There was an ear-shattering explosion and, Frost's head still ringing with it, he looked up, the tank stopped dead, a fireball bursting upward from it, then another explosion—the rounds for the turret gun—ripping through the pre-dawn sky. Frost, half stumbling, was already on his feet, racing back into the higher rocks. There was another explosion and Frost looked toward the beach—there was a wall of fire in the long trench made for the beach defenders—the napalm had been ignited, that was the signal to begin the beach landing. One more tank still out there, Frost, Davison, Timmons and the other two men started through the rocks, hunting for it somewhere below them on the beach. The impenetrable wall of flames as long as it held would keep the Ramon troops from reaching the beach—only the one remaining Soviet tank could perhaps make it across and because of that, Frost had to find it.

The naval bombardment, such as it was, was already starting, the target the wall of flame from the napalmed trench, the sound of the gun on the deck of the Angel One unmistakable. Frost stared across the flames, seeing another flash of light, this from the Angel Three, a loud whistling sound high on the darkness, then an explosion on the beach—the tank they had captured on the island of Sabot had been rigged to fire from the deck of the Angel Three and it too had joined in the bombardment. Suddenly, Frost saw the last Soviet tank, and as he'd predicted it was started toward the burning trench to cross

166

onto the beach side. The sun was already coming up over the mountains and jungle inland and in the half light now Frost could see the first of the invasion fleet of motorized rubber launches and gunboats starting toward shore. If the tank crossed the flames it would destroy most of the invasion fleet before it landed.

Frost, shouting to Timmons to follow him, rasped then to Davison, "Get your tankers to go after that—we've got to stop it."

Davison said nothing, then with his two unemployed tank drivers started back across the rocks. Frost and Timmons started after the tank themselves.

"Sir—what the bloody hell are we going to do to stop that?" Timmons shouted, his Greasegun spitting fire as a half dozen of the Ramon troops came out of the rocks and toward them.

Frost, dropping to one knee fired his own subgun, the weapon going dry, then Frost swinging the CAR-16 into position and continuing to fire. On his feet again, Frost shouted back to Timmons, "We'll improvise—don't worry!" Racing across the sand toward the tank, Frost shouted again to Timmons, "Get that M-79 going to draw the tank's fire—maybe we can delay it!"

As Timmons fired the first High Explosive grenade, the grenade merely bouncing off the Russian armor as it exploded, no mark even on the tank, Frost started lobbing some of the grenades from his belt, knowing that like the grenades from the M-79, they were useless against

167

the leviathan.

But the tank stopped rolling forward, rolling a foot or so backward as its settled on the sand, the turret gun swinging all the way around and toward Frost and Timmons, both men now crouched behind some low rocks. "Kiss your fanny good-bye," Frost shouted to the Britisher, then suddenly there was another rumbling sound and Frost looked to his right, one of the captured tanks—it had to be, Frost almost prayed—coming across the beach, its turret sweeping toward the remaining Ramon-controlled tank, the turret gun on the Ramon tank then sweeping away from Frost and Timmons, firing, the ground trembling with the sound and the force, the ground in front of the captured tank exploding, the captured tank stopping, its turret gun swinging into position. The Ramon-held tank fired again and so did the captured tank, almost simultaneously. The combined explosions made Frost's ears ring, the light almost blinding. As the fireballs drifted into the greying sky, both tanks were dead.

"Damnit," Frost rasped, then started out across the beach into a dead run toward the far rocks. Timmons and Frost reached the rocks and climbed them, on the other side the rattle of small arms fire already clear, Davison and two of his men pinned down, one of the captured tanks rolling in. Frost shouldered his CAR-16, firing the weapon full auto into the concentration of Ramon forces, drawing their gunfire away from Davison and into the rocks toward himself and

Timmons. Frost shouted to the Britisher, "Timmons—get the M-79 going down there—hurry, man!"

The shotgun-like grenade launcher broke open, Timmons loaded, closed the action and de-activated the automatic safety, then fired, the weapon hard against his shoulder, the grenade impacting in the center of the Ramon lines, screams, cries filling the air over the noise of the blast. The captured tank was rolling up, its turret gun firing, driving the Ramon troops now back toward the still flaming trench.

Frost swung up the binoculars, just focusing the right tube in the gathering light and looking beyond the wall of flame—the first of the rubber boats had hit the beach, and men were clambering over the sides of the gunboats and converted pleasure boats, wading through chest deep water, some of them already firing. The gunboats themselves were firing their heavy machineguns as some of the Ramon forces made it across the lowering flames of the trench or worked themselves up the beach and around the flames to engage the invaders.

Frost, Timmons, Davison and the two men who had been designated to operate the now destroyed tanks, began working themselves high up into the rocks, Frost settling into a notch there, the sun at his back, the scoped Colt assault rifle with the stock fully extended to his shoulder, the selector set to semi-auto fire. Frost settled the three power scope's crosshairs on one of Ramon's officers, perhaps one hundred and twenty yards off, then Frost's finger touched the trigger, the man going down, both hands springing to his chest. Timmons, behind and to Frost's left, was firing the grenade launcher—Frost could hear it each time the grenades whooshed from the shotgun like M-79, the grenades impacting on the sand, cratering it, claiming the lives of the Communist soldiers nearby. Frost fired again, missing, then made a quick follow-up shot, nailing a non-com not far from the fallen officer. A smile crossed Frost's lips—ever since the loss of the eye he never had to worry about squinting his left eye shut when he fired a rifle—rather like the classic cure for athlete's foot, he thought—cut off the leg.

Frost tore his eye from the scope, glancing to his left, beyond the burnt-out trench fire, his mercenary troops swarming up onto the beach now by the hundreds, the bombardment from off shore stopping to avoid hitting the attackers. The four captured tanks were chewing their way across the beachhead now, rolling over pillboxes and machinegun emplacements. There was some mortar fire still, but it wasn't heavy enough to be pinning down the invasion force.

Frost turned back to the scoped rifle at his shoulder, firing down into the Ramon troops at a fever pitch—victory, at least a temporary victory, was at hand.

Chapter Nineteen

Some small arms fire still persisted from the rocks high above the beach and almost into the jungle beyond, but it was a harrassing fire—the beachhead had been taken—Frost looked at his watch—two hours earlier, by ten A.M. By the shoreline and beyond the rocks, it was safe to move about and there a tent had been set up as command post, Marina having come ashore to join the troops, a radio set up now to attempt to contact the army of Commacho's nephew, Adolpho.

"I have them, I have them," the Angel One radio operator shouted, racing across the sand toward Frost, Marina a few yards ahead of him, her bare feet in the surf.

Frost started running toward the tent, Marina passing him and Frost smiling, almost laughing as she did—the barefoot dark haired girl, her jeans rolled up to her knees, sand clinging to her wet feet and calves. She beat Frost into the tent and by the time Frost reached it she was already on the radio, the set switched over into the speaker.

"English," she half shouted.

"Si," a voice crackled back. "Aqui esta Adolpho," and there was silence as the radio operator somewhere off in the jungle apparently handed Adolpho Commacho the microphone.

"This is Adolpho Commacho—Marina?"

"Si—yes, Adolpho. We have taken the beachhead at point Bravo."

"Is Capitan Frost with you, the one-eyed man?"

Marina didn't answer for a moment, then some of the breathless enthusiasm gone from her voice, she said, "Yes—but there is no time for—"

"I am not a boy—you do not need to tell me this. But later—then he and I. We are a day's march from your position. We have been waiting for almost a week. There is an air base near-by—my men will try and take it soon. But they have just launched a fighter squadron and I must assume it is going toward your position. Your anti-aircraft guns are emplaced?"

"We have some equipment," the girl said into the microphone.

Frost was glad the girl evidently realized the

172

enemy was quite probably monitoring the communications—and Frost assumed Commacho was aware of this as well. Adolpho's young sounding voice came back on the air. "We shall fight our way toward your beachhead, then sweep overland. We are gaining much popular support, our army swells its ranks with each hour. Ramon is filth here."

Frost thought he heard something, then stepped to the end of the tent, looking up into the greyish blue of the sky—he did hear something, though he could see nothing. Planes. Frost wheeled, "Kiss Adolpho good-bye for me," he rasped, "and tell him thanks for the tip on the fighters—they're coming."

Frost tore from the tent, running across the sand, the CAR slung across his back, the KG-9 slung at his left side. Shouting over his shoulder, he hollered back to the tent. "Alert the ships to get ready for an attack!" He searched the beachhead for Timmons, seeing the Britisher, shouting to him, "Get those riflemen ready—air attack in about two minutes!"

Frost raced up toward the rocks, some of the machineguns emplaced there, finding Davison, in charge of the beachhead defenses, "Davison! Aircraft, fighters! Get ready."

Frost started back across the sand toward the tent, stopping in mid-stride, staring upward into the sky, then throwing himself down to the sand near a clump of rocks, the first of the fighters streaking across the sky, its guns roaring, the sand chewing up as if the ground itself were ripping asunder. Frost pushed himself to his feet and raced across the sand toward the tent, ducking inside, "Get that radio protected and get the hell out of this tent—now," then Frost grabbed Marina, her mouth half-open as if to speak. "Shut up," he rasped, then grabbing her right wrist in his left hand, the CAR slung forward now to fire, he started out of the tent. The next Soviet fighter was making its pass and Frost, dragging the girl behind him, started running across the sand toward the rocks, hearing the roar of the guns, the crack of air over the foil of the wings, the jets on afterburners. Frost dove for the rocks, dragging the girl with him, the air crackling overhead, the sand, the rocks, spitting into the air as the aircraft machinegun slugs tore into them. Frost popped himself up in a niche of rocks, the CAR-16 to his shoulder, the scope covers ripped away, his finger working the trigger in three shot bursts, aiming at the next Soviet fighterplane starting a run across the beach. The makeshift anti-aircraft guns aboard Angels One and Three were firing now, the machineguns on the beach at full cyclic rate, Timmons' brigade of riflemen peppering the sky against the Soviet fighters.

The fighters massed again for attack, circling low and in a wedge formation streaking down toward the beach, their guns blazing, missiles this time impacting against the beach. One of the tanks was returning fire, and one of the turret guns connected with the second jet behind the leader, the plane exploding in a huge, black and yellow fireball, the other jet fighters veering off. Davison's LAWS rocket teams started firing as the jets streaked low across the beach again, their own missiles impacting perilously close to the tanks, but the LAWS rockets fired in salvo soaring skyward toward the jet fighters' low angle of flight, one of the jets taking a hit on the starboard wing, the plane soaring up, backing on itself, exploding in mid-air.

Frost was still firing the Colt rifle in his hands, the gun coming up empty, then changing sticks. He started firing again, aiming at the transparent canopy of the nearest jet as it streaked over the beach. He shouted over the roar, "Go for the first one—the canopy."

The riflemen in Timmons' company of men started firing again, Frost directing his fire as they did toward the canopy of the nearest jet. As it streaked past, a missile impacting into the command tent, the canopy seemed to crash, the plane veering right and left as though waving its wings to someone on the ground below, then the plane veering hard to port and heading out low over the water, nosing into—"My God," Frost rasped.

The Soviet-made jet was going to hit Angel Three. "No," he shouted, starting to his feet and still firing as he ran into the surf. The jet impacted, a huge fireball rising over the afterdeck of Angel Three, then an explosion and another fireball. Frost cursed, then rammed a fresh thirty-round magazine into the CAR, the last of the fighters screaming along the beach, firing its missiles and machineguns. "Get that bastard," Frost shouted, then the LAWS rockets in Davison's group, the riflemen under Timmons, all of them concentrated their fire on the last fighter, the fighter coming inexorably over the sand, Frost just standing there, shooting his gun until it was empty, snatching the KG-9—he knew it was useless now—and ramming back the bolt, holding the gun by the ventilated front handguard, his right hand working the trigger, on his knees now shooting as the jet streaked toward him. LAWS rockets, rounds from one of the tank turret guns, rifle bullets pouring skyward at it. Frost, the KG-9 at his hip, was just firing now to keep mentally from giving up. The plane suddenly seemed to shudder, then pulled up, firing a last burst from its machineguns, Frost hitting the sand finally, the surf washing across his face as he looked up, the jet streaking skyward then, without anything visibly wrong with it, suddenly exploding. Frost pushed himself up on his hands, staring seaward to the Angel Three—it was afire and listing in the stern. Shouting as he got to his feet, he rasped, "Radioman—get their situation, tell them we're sending boats out—hurry!"

Chapter Twenty

"Adolpho estimates he is eighteen hours away—he cannot give us his exact position because perhaps the communications are monitored. He thinks they are."

"Yeah—well, that only stands to reason," Frost rasped, lighting a cigarette, sitting so the surf lapped up at his bare toes—his feet ached somehow.

"How many men did we lose when the jet hit the deck of Angel Three?"

"About fifteen guys—surprisingly little," Frost told her. "Fifteen too many though. A lot of them were crew. Got two of the big machineguns, too." Frost as watching the sunset and almost resented the intrusion—he was watching the Angel Three as well. An hour earlier, they had given up on the pumping efforts and were letting her go down.

Things were going to be crowded, Frost thought, aboard the Angel One and on the beach.

If they had to evacuate now, there would not be enough room unless they wanted to pack themselves like sardines or ditch all the equipment on the beach and deep six the rest. "Reminds me of the story they tell of Cortez, burning his ships behind him so his men had no choice but to conquer Mexico—they couldn't return. A lot of those old armies were mercenaries, really. Men who fought for pay. My guys are doing pretty well, aren't they?"

"Why do they fight so hard? Like you, they hate the Communistas?"

"Si," Frost sighed. "Like me they hate the Communistas. And, like me, I guess they get involved. You can't help it really." And Frost gestured behind him to the beachhead, "I think almost every man out there would throttle Ramon to death with his bare hands given half a chance—we've lost too many guys. This isn't just somebody else's war now—it's our war. We want to win it I think more than you do."

"Do you think we are winning?" the girl asked softly.

"Yes, oddly enough," Frost told her, feeling tired, old and half-dead as he watched the sun and the tired freighter, Angel Three, sinking in almost perfect unison. "That sort of duel we had with the Soviet fighters was a morale booster in a way, despite what happened to Angel Three. We proved to ourselves we could take and defeat anything they threw against us—even air power. Yeah—I think we'll win. We could still blow it, or Ramon could pull something out of his hat. I figure those tanks were airlifted here and if I'm wrong and there's some way to get tanks overland and he's got lots of them to play with and they come rolling down here, we lose. Or, if they send a hundred fighters or even a couple dozen at us at once, we lose. But I don't know how much equipment they have to throw away. Any word on the airbase when you talked to Adolpho?"

"Yes," the girl said. It was awkward not being able to talk to one of the Commanders technically under you, Frost realized. But Commacho would not talk with Frost—Frost had tried, then simply told Adolpho Commacho to go to hell. "Adolpho says his men have the airbase under attack and it is going well."

"That doesn't mean a damned thing," Frost told her quietly.

"He could be losing and if he thinks Ramon's forces are listening he'd say it was going well. Well, let's hope he's telling it to us pretty straight. I guess we'll see."

"So we wait for Adolpho?"

"Got no choice," Frost told her. "Holding position with the numbers and equipment we have is one thing, but taking off across that jungle and storming the capital is something else.

179

If Commacho really has the manpower he says he has, and if he really is getting the popular support, then fine—we'll make it across the mountains and through the jungle and we'll be knocking on Ernesto Ramon's little door and knocking on his little Communist head too. May start a popular past-time—plant a dictator instead of a tree, something like that. We'll see.''

"Do you want something to eat—the cook tent is operating?''

"Sure,'' Frost told her, smiling. There was an audible gurgling sound as the bow of the Angel Three began to sink, the beach suddenly darkening as the sun began to sink as well. Frost used the outsides of his boot socks to dust the dried sand from his feet, then replaced the socks and the combat boots, not bothering to lace them fully. "What's the special tonight?''

"In the cook tent?'' she smiled.

"You know,'' Frost sighed. "Anybody ever tell you that aside from a fine intellect and a beautiful body you also have an exceedingly dirty mind?'' He grabbed her, his left arm encircling her waist. Taking one more glance as the bow of Angel Three disappeared into the waves, he started with her across the sand toward the yellow buglight swaying inside the cook tent. There was still some scattered small arms fire, but that was least of his worries now.

Chapter Twenty-one

There was an organized, almost suicidal frontal assault, an Asian-style human wave attack at midnight, mortars exploding along the beach front, Frost and his various commanders supporting their own defenses as best as possible. Frost read in the faces of his men that they were almost sickened by the bloodshed as wave after wave of Ramon's troops came, streaking across the naked beach and dying under the withering automatic weapons fire from the mercenary unit.

There was another message from Adolpho—he was now twelve hours away, encountering heavy resistance but punching through. With the receipt of the message, Frost at once understood the Ramon plan, the Communist strategy. They were simply trying to keep Frost and his men in place, then stop Commacho's Army from linking up. Once that was accomplished they could take their time about liquidating the invading army on the beach. That was why resistance had been so comparatively light. Marina had forgotten to ask Adolpho about the fight for the airbase and Adolpho had volunteered no fresh information. That sounded bad to Frost.

By two in the morning, Frost finally got some sleep, leaving instructions with Davison, Timmons and the others to awaken him for the slightest reason.

Opening his eye, he glanced at his watch—eight A.M. It looked on the beach like something from a World War Two movie, men carrying rifles, tanks and equipment everywhere. The surf lapped at the shore and it was even cool, a light mist hung over the sand and the surf. There was again the intermittent harassing fire but things were generally calm.

Frost had almost gotten to the point of not noticing it.

Wandering down by the surf after securing a cup of coffee from the cook tent, Frost saw Marina, saw her waving at him from the cook tent. He looked at the coffee, then tossed it into the surf and, the empty cup in hand, he ran across the beach toward the tent—he hoped this one lasted longer than the previous one which had been destroyed by one of the rockets from the Soviet jet fighters.

"It is Adolpho!"

Frost looked at the girl, found a coffee pot in the corner of the tent and went over to it. "Fine—talk to Adolpho—and don't forget to find out about that airbase, huh?"

Feeling the rough stubble on his face, Frost turned a chair around with his feet and straddled it, staring at the radio speaker as if he could somehow picture Adolpho Commacho's face by looking at it.

"Si, Adolpho?"

Frost loved their formal radio procedure, he thought. Whatever happened to good old prowords?

"Si—we are now about eight hours away from you—we have been slowed down but they are not stopping us. We have taken the airbase and will soon have the Russian fighter aircraft sent here by Castro in the air, helping in securing our victory." Frost, his sense of humor not the best when he first awakened, stood up and saluted the loudspeaker. Marina smiled and waved him down. Laughing, sipping at his coffee and lighting a cigarette, Frost listened as Adolpho continued ". . . resistance gets any heavier. We are forging ahead. As we come nearer the beach, I will alert you."

"Marina," Frost rasped, "tell him to get some way for those fighters to announce themselves as our guys so we don't shoot 'em down."

"Adolpho," the girl asked into the microphone. "How will we know if fighters come over the beachhead that they are yours?"

There was laughter a moment, crackling

183

through the speaker, "You will know—I have provided for this—do not fear. Wait—" and the radio went dead a moment, then there was a crackle and the voice sounded somehow older, deeper, "I have just received word from our intelligence sources. Castro has sent four thousand "volunteers" to the capital—they have already begun landing to aid Ramon's troops."

"Ohh, that's just wonderful, wonderful," Frost said, shaking his head. "Enough of this crap," and he stood up walking over to the radio. He took the microphone from Marina. "Adolpho—this is Frost. Now, dammit, talk to me—otherwise you can kiss this thing good-bye and I'm taking Marina and everything I can't take I'll junk so you can't use it—Frost over."

The radio speaker crackled with silence for a moment, then, "This is Adolpho Commacho. Si. I agree. We must talk."

"Good," Frost said into the microphone. "Now—when you get within an hour or so of here do the following: contact me, give me an approximate position and twenty minutes later send up a flare and I'll confirm the exact location by radio. My people will link up with you. And, if any of Ramon's people are listening, fine—take this back to Ernesto for me," Frost rasped into the microphone. "Once we link up, he can bring in all the Castro whimps he wants and we'll make meat out of 'em—and you can quote that. Frost out!"

Frost handed the microphone back to Marina—his coffee was cold and he spilled it into

184

the sand outside the tent and poured another cup, his stomach rumbling because he needed breakfast . . .

Noon, then one o'clock came and went and still no word came from Adolpho Commacho's Army—it numbered upwards of two thousand men, Frost had been given to believe. And if what Commacho said were true about the volunteers it could have increased to three thousand men or more by now. With the captured weapons and extra arms from the ship Angel One, it would not be difficult, Frost reasoned, to field a reasonably well-armed force of thirty-five hundred to throw against the Ramon units and the Castro support troops. There was going to be a major battle—Frost realized that and the thought did not excite him. If they picked up a thousand more men, armed them, trained them to where the numerical advantage of the combined Ramon and Castro forces were not too great, there would be a chance. The Ramon Army was estimated at eight thousand men at present strength.

Frost sat near the radio tent, waiting. Davison was still in charge of the beach defenses and Frost was sending Timmons with three hundred men into the jungle to link up with Ramon—as soon as they got the word. But the word wasn't coming.

By two P.M., Frost was pacing down at the surf, looking back to the radio tent every moment or so. There should have been something, he told himself. The harassing fire had still not increased nor was there anything to indicate that Adolpho's Army approached.

"Capitan Frost! Capitan!" The thin faced radio operator ran from the tent, toward Frost and Frost, seeing him, started running toward the tent himself, the two men meeting at the approximate middleground. The radio operator ran back beside Frost. "Commacho has called."

Frost swung against the pole near the tent flap, half-stumbling toward the radio, grabbing the microphone. "Adolpho!"

"Si—We are near—less than two miles I judge—large enemy force between us. Send your men," then the radio went dead.

Frost turned to the operator, "What hap—"

"He gave me his position first."

"Fine," Frost snapped. "Give it to Timmons and get it on a map for me," he added, already running across the sand, shouting, "Timmons!"

"Sir!"

Frost stopped in mid-stride, saw the radio man running toward the beefy Englishman. "Two miles or less—get cracking. You need reinforcements—large enemy force between you."

"Right you are, sir!"

The big Britisher was streaking across the sand, already rousting his men. Frost turned, sensing Marina approaching—she threw her arms around his neck and Frost swung her off the ground. The Army was all but one.

A jet fighter streaked over the beach. Scrawled along the base of the fuselage in black paint in Spanish were the words, "Death to the Tyrant!"

Chapter Twenty-two

The float plane cast a fast moving shadow on the green jungle canopy below them as Frost stared down on it, the darkness moving so swiftly but Frost sitting in the plane itself having little sensation of the motion. The plane was an old, much worked-on Beechcraft—the modern Beechcraft planes weren't generally suited to float use. Frost knew several men who flew, pilots whose lives depended on what they knew about aircraft as much as Frost's life sometimes depended on what he knew about guns or knives. To a man, they swore by Beechcraft as an outfit making solidly built aircraft that wore like iron and handled like sportscars. Frost had always promised himself that someday he would learn to fly and he understood that for maybe fifty thousand dollars he could get into a good, used twin—frame time in planes like these, Frost had been told, meant little. A ten or fifteen-year-old plane could be as good as a new one if properly maintained.

Frost looked back down at the jungle—the dream of learning to fly, of owning a plane—all his dreams were on the backburner now as he crossed the jungle and mountains toward the Atlantic Coast of Monte Azul. This was the last of the job—but it might be the last of everything Frost knew.

After Timmons had fought his way toward Adolpho Commacho, then Frost had brought in reinforcements and the two armies had finally linked, there had been a war council—a strategy session and Frost had finally made his decision. Commacho's Army was much larger than Frost had imagined—six thousand men, half or whom were well-trained. With the surviving members of Frost's invasion Army, that made nearly seven thousand troops and there was the promise of picking up still additional volunteers from among the people of Monte Azul. All told, the counter-revolutionary Army supporting Marina Aguillara-Garcia was strong enough to fight the Ernesto Ramon Communist Army and the four thousand Castro "volunteers." But to insure victory, Frost had decided he would best serve the "cause" by doing what he did best. He disliked moving vast numbers of men—he had always excelled at small unit tactics, always felt that in

188

most situations a dozen of the best men could accomplish a task all but impossible for two hundred average soldiers. Now, with eleven men Frost himself had picked, trained closely with for three days, eleven men he trusted, Frost was flying across the jungle while Commacho and Marina led their Army overland against the capital. Frost would land in the Atlantic, off the coast of Playa Del Sur and the town of San Luis where the big battle between Marina's father and his old friend who had gone over to the Communists had taken place, the seaside town where Frost had seen President Aguillara-Garcia, seen Marina's father so terribly moved by the starving children with crooked limbs, balding heads and swollen bellies. It was there, Frost reflected, that he decided what kind of a man Marina's father had been, that he had decided it was more than just a job—what happened in Monte Azul.

Once landed, they would strike out for the capital, by car, by foot, however necessary. They would penetrate the capital and—Frost looked back into the cabin, feeling the plane beginning to descend. Frost, from his seat in the starboard side of the fuselage, felt almost as if the twelve-foot floats beneath the wings had to be skimming along on the green jungle canopy itself as they dropped elevation—but the plane moved smoothly. Frost unstrapped himself from the seat and worked his way forward, feeling the slight forward sloping of the floor of the fuselage, letting himself into the pilot's cabin, staring over the pilot's shoulder. The jungle was starting to thin ahead of them, some granite outcroppings already showing—for the first time Frost realized why the small central American nation was called Monte Azul—"blue mountain." The granite itself was slightly blue tinged, and with green lichens growing on the rocks below them now as they swept toward the sea, it was hard to imagine the ugliness of warfare in such an Eden-like land.

The ocean was fast approaching now and in the distance off the portside wingtip Frost could see the meager streets and buildings of San Luis, principal city of Playa del Sur—South Beach in English, he thought. As Presidente Aguillara-Garcia had learned when Frost had been with him, Playa del Sur suffered from neglect. On the coast, a day's overland journey from the capital, populated mainly with what a hundred years ago would have been called peasants, from what Frost could see and what Commacho's nephew Adolpho had told them, it was still neglected. As the young Commacho had described it, there was nothing there to steal, so no one bothered.

Frost watched, mystified, as the pilot manipulated the controls in some magical way that made the float plane circle over the sand of the beach and down low over the water, then arc back toward the sand, the plane seeming already to be touching the water. There was something like a skidding sound, but somehow different as the plane touched against the surface—Frost felt a shudder in the plane, realizing it had landed. But the plane still moved. Frost stared out past

190

the vacant co-pilot's seat, the plane skimming now over the tiny waves, the white sand of Playa del Sur coming up beyond the propellerless nose of the plane. Frost looked back to the pilot. He was thoroughly confused now—the steering wheel-like control the pilot held remained motionless yet somehow, as the pilot's feet moved, the plane wheeled almost 180 degrees so the portside fronted the beach, now some twenty or thirty yards distant.

"Should be shallow enough here," the man said. Frost looked at him, shaking his head. "What's the matter," the American asked.

"CIA—right?"

"Well—let's just say I'm helping Commacho out of the goodness of my heart."

"Let's say CIA," Frost smiled. "How long does it take to become a pilot?"

"Not too long—then all you gotta do is practice."

"Wow," Frost said with genuine feeling, then started aft to roust together his eleven man team. "Edison," Frost shouted, the blonde-haired, grey-mustachioed American already half out of his seat. "Get Kujinama and start off-loading the equipment to the rest of us," then Frost turned toward Keagle, the CIA pilot, the portside fuselage cargo door opening, the sound of water lapping against the floats the only sound besides the shuffling of Frost's men inside the aircraft.

"Well," Frost sighed, "Faint heart, etc.," then crouching down, he dropped out through the cargo door into the water, the water up to his crotch. He turned and shouted back into the plane to Givens, Timmons' friend from London, "Givens—toss me my gear," and Frost took his pack, his pistol belt, the musette bag and his rifle, holding them over his head as he started shoreward, Svernbjorg, the red-headed Swede who was a veteran of every African campaign of the last dozen years, already jumping from the plane, a link-belt-fed M-60 Machinegun cradled in his arms, the link belts festooned on his massive, iron-presser shoulders.

Frost reached the sand, set his pack and the musette bag down and strapped on the pistol belt, then took the CAR-16 hybrid he carried and eared back the bolt, chambering the top round from the thirty-shot magazine the Colt carried and moved up along the beach—the sooner the unloading was done and the plane gone, the sooner Frost knew he and the eleven others could slip into the sparse forest fronting the beach and make their way into the town of San Luis and be on their way . . .

The meeting that night following Commacho and Frost's defeat of the Ramon force between them had been bitter—Frost and Commacho at each other's throats. Because, Frost realized, young Commacho wanted him dead. Finally, when Frost had come up with the idea of the commando raid on the capital to be timed with an attack on the capital itself, Commacho had revealed his American military advisors—and the plane that could land in the water on the Pacific side and fly across the jungle to drop Frost and his team on the Atlantic side. That night, Frost had begun selection of the strike force.

Moving through the woods paralleling a dirt and gravel road toward the town of San Luis now, Frost reviewed the plan. Penetrate the capital, reach the Presidential Palace which he knew so well, enter through a secret entrance Marina had told him of, an entrance which had never shown up on the plans of the structure he had reviewed when first taking charge of Aguillara-Garcia's security. Locate Ramon, hopefully too locate the head of the Castro "volunteer" force—liquidate them both. "Simple," Frost muttered to himself, stopping by the edge of the tree line and staring up along the road toward the town. There were perhaps three, maybe four guards by the road, lounging there, two of them smoking. Frost couldn't quite tell if the fourth man were a guard—he was beating a dog with a stick and he wore no uniform shirt, his back toward Frost's position.

The dog, yellowish in color pegged out between two staked chains so it could barely move, was small, and seemingly harmless enough. It appeared, Frost thought, that the man just enjoyed beating something.

"Ve go round?" Svernbjorg asked.

Frost looked at the red-headed Swede, saying, his voice low, "They're going to notice us as soon as we steal a car or truck, right? Let's let 'em notice us now. Take two guys with you and circle the town, make sure it's as empty as it looks, then fire a flare if it's okay. I'm killing that sucker," and Frost pointed to the man beating the dog with the big, thorn-knuckled stick.

"Ya—I like dat," the Swede smiled, then disappeared into the trees, the M-60 with a full hundred-round box under it looking as light as a feather in the man's arm, the spare link belts worn on his shoulders like a woman might wear pearls around her neck.

Frost sat at the edge of the tree line, watching the beating, listening to the animal yelping. It seemed like an eternity to him. There was a noise, like a small gauge shotgun shell discharging and Frost looked skyward toward the end of the long street and past the wharves—a starburst flare. Frost moved the selector switch on the CAR-16 to auto and shouted to his men as he got to his feet, "The one beating the dog is mine!"

Frost ran down into the road, the Ramon guards already starting to turn from staring at the flare in the sky, staring toward the far end of the town where Svernbjorg's heavy machinegun was already beating a steady rhythm. The shirtless man turned, the stick still in his hands, the half unconscious dog lying in the dust and Frost, several paces ahead of Givens and the rest of the men, braced into a classic assault position. He glared at the unarmed Ramon guard and shouted, "Habla Ingles?"

"Si," the man said, his head cocked slightly back, a look of indignation in his eyes.

"Good—you're a son of a bitch," and Frost

194

fired a three-round burst from the assault rifle ripping a diagonal slash in the shirtless man's naked chest and neck, the indignation in the man's eyes replaced by a look of astonishment as the man fell to the ground, the stick dropping from his right hand, blood on it from the dog. Frost walked forward, the other three men already down. Frost signaled his men forward. They walked ahead through the streets. Givens, a qualified medic, had then seen if something could be done for the dog. The gunfire subsided completely as Givens joined Frost again, nodding his head negative about the dog. Frost heard a rumbling, turned, spotted a military two and one-half ton truck—U.S. surplus?—rolling down the dusty street toward them. Frost started signalling his men back into the shelter of nearby doorways as the truck slowed. Through the dust, almost silhouetted against the main part of the cloud, Frost could see the Japanese mercenary Kujinama, hanging from the passenger side door, waving an M-16, grinning from ear to ear.

The truck squealed to a full stop, Svernbjorg jumping down from the driver's side, then gesturing toward the truck, "She okay?"

"She fine," Frost smiled, then turned to the others, shouting, "Pile on!"

Frost squeezed into the front seat with the Japanese and the big Swede, the other nine men and the equipment in the back. Frost looked at his watch, then looked back at the sleepy fishing village of San Luis on Playa del Sur. Perhaps no one bothered with the town because the town did not bother with itself.

Chapter Twenty-three

Frost and the others had stopped some twenty miles outside on the town of San Luis and changed uniforms—plain dark green fatigues with a brassard or patch of the left shoulder with the purple and black banner on the Communist Government of Monte Azul and dark green baseball caps. Since the military in Monte Azul used a variety of sidearms, Frost and the others kept their own, and the standard issue weapon was still the M-16 carried over from the days of Marina's father. Frost read the nametag on his uniform—he was Major Ceballos, with cloth oak leaves on his collar to prove it. He had stripped away the eyepatch as well and donned sunglasses, these common too in the Ramon military. Replacing his obviously American Camels with a cigar, he thought he completed the picture. The other men similarly clad—Kujinama was the only problem—they had remounted the truck and continued along the road toward the capital. By nightfall, they stopped fifty miles outside the capital with clear road ahead of them. If their luck held, Frost thought, they could roll in all the way, at least to the outskirts of the city. They had encountered one Ramon patrol with the vehicles heading the opposite way toward the province of Playa del Sur. It had merely slowed, one of the drivers had waved and Frost and the big Swede, now occupying the front seat, had waved back. The Swede's coloring was not a problem. He was deeply tanned and red hair was not unknown in Monte Azul.

A fireless campsite far off the road, then a restless night's sleep for Frost and his eleven men, then an on-the-run breakfast and back to the truck before dawn—and as the sun began rising behind them, Frost, driving now because he knew the city, downshifted the big deuce-and-a-half. He did a fast, hard right onto the sloping dirt road leading toward the main highway that ran from the city past the relatively modern airport. Frost remembered a gunfight there with terrorists as—how long ago had it been he thought—he had led the U.S. Embassy staff, Marina and her father and stepmother and his own men out of the city to escape the Communists. He smiled, wondering what had happened to Anna, Aguillara-Garcia's widow. Frost

197

thought that he had never met a more sexually obsessed woman in his life.

The dirt road leading down to the highway was steep and Frost slowed the truck to keep better control. Their good luck had to soon end; he knew that. They would encounter Ramon security forces—but when? There had been considerable activity on the road all the previous day—as if Ramon had been calling in units from the countryside to support the defenders of the capital and for that reason, Frost thought, he and the other eleven men seemed less suspicious—like everyone else they were on their way to fight Adolpho Commacho, Marina and that horrible American mercenary, Hank Frost. Frost smiled at that—he didn't think he was really all that horrible. "Sincere," he whispered to himself.

"What you say?" Svernbjorg asked.

Not a thing, pal," Frost told the red-haired man. "Not a thing. Shout back for me to the rest of the guys—we're going to be hitting that paved highway pretty quick now and we've got to start hitting Ramon security once we do."

But Frost stopped the truck and pulled along the side of the road before the Swede could shout. Below him less than a half-mile away Frost could see tbe highway and beyond that on the far side the airport. He ran the details of the plan through this mind again. Penetrate the Palace, get Ramon who would most certainly be hiding out there for his own security, perhaps get the leader of the Castro volunteers too. Do it all at a pre-arranged time when Marina and Com-macho's nephew would launch their attack against the city, Adolpho Commacho personally leading a small, airborne strike force that would land on the Palace grounds and with Frost's men already in place secure the area and allow Com-macho to declare victory. Very simple, Frost thought.

"Why stopping?" the Swede asked.

Frost turned and looked at the man, thinking that his English made him sound more like an Indian out of a 1950s television western. "Time to execute the secret elements of my master plan."

"What is master plan?"

"Well," Frost said. "You'll see in a minute."

Frost killed the engine on the truck and got out, checking his rifle, staring silently at the road and the airport beyond. He could see some figures moving about on the airport runways, a few planes, a few helicopters. He walked back around the side of the truck, calling to Svern-bjorg to get down and join him. Frost stopped, the profile of the truck obscuring the airport from view. Turning around, he looked up at the ten men in the back of the deuce-and-a-half, say-ing, "Okay—a little change in plans."

"What?" It was Belford, one of the black mercenaries, a man Frost had worked with once before in Africa.

"Yeah Frank," Frost said, looking at Belford, then at the others. "A little change. I figured all along that Commacho's nephew might not be shootin' us the straight dope, maybe be lookin' to get us knocked off or something. Well, it looks like he's been straight, but even so, I just get bad vibes about driving into the capital down there, ditching the truck and going over the wall into the Presidential Palace. Sounds too simple, too easy. Stuff like that's always scary.''

"Then—ahh, what do we do, Frost?"

Frost looked at Kujinama. "Well, like I said, I planned around it. We can get into the Palace another way, a little more spectacularly. Marina gave me a rundown on the Presidential Palace, including a secret entrance and exit I hadn't known about. I figured if there was one, there had to be more than one—you know, they come in pairs?''

Givens, the Englishman, began to grin, getting Frost's double entendre. "So,'' Frost went on, "I found out about another way in and out. And when I picked you guys, I intentionally picked guys who knew how to rappel, knew something about airborne operations and,'' and Frost looked at Frank Belford, "I also picked somebody with helicopter experience. We are going down into that little airport over there, steal ourselves a nice sized chopper, then fly in over the palace, carefully avoiding getting shot down. We rappel down to the roof, some of us stay on the roof to play shoot 'em up with Ramon's troops, a few of us go inside through a passage that lets out in the old attic just under the roofline, then we get Ramon and whoever else looks important, then Frank,'' and Frost looked back at Belford, "flies down and picks us up if we need it and we hit the trail—I don't want Adolpho Commacho trapping us in the Palace unless the shooting has stopped.''

"You're crazy man,'' Belford smiled.

"That's the nicest thing anybody's said to me all day,'' Frost responded. Then, "Any questions? Hmm?''

"Yeah—you think any of us is gettin' out of there in one piece, Captain?'' It was Carl Finch—"Fingers Finch'' they called him, Frost remembered, because he had six fingers on his left hand.

"Yeah, Fingers,'' Frost smiled. "If I didn't think we'd get out, I'd just send you.'' There was a round of laughter, then almost instantaneous, unanimous silence. Frost said, his voice low, the words coming slowly, "Yeah—maybe not all of us, but we've got a good chance. See—I'm timing us to start our attack five minutes after Commacho's forces hit the town—the last thing anybody is going to worry about is a bunch of nuts landing on the roof of the palace. Especially since we've got one other trick up the the old sleeve.''

"Which is?'' Frank Belford asked, lighting a ciagarette.

"Which is,'' Frost smiled. "One of the guys we killed when we linked up with Commacho's people had a code book on him. That Company man who dropped us outside San Luis in Playa del Sur? Well, he's getting on the radio just about now,'' and Frost glanced at his watch, "and warning Ramon of an attack against the

Presidential Palace and that a special commando team will be sent into guard the palace along with the regulars who are already there. Now, Ramon's people are obviously going to figure that's a trick—so, when we lead the people from the airport over there after us once we steal the chopper, they are going to come storming into the Palace Grounds, they are going to be expected and they are going to get shot at. Then we move in. Should buy us enough confusion to hit the roof. Maybe it won't—we'll see. Now,'' and Frost stepped closer to the truck, "here's what we do.'' As Frost began to outline the plan to the eleven men of his commando team, he found himself thinking half-aloud, "This has got to be the dumbest thing I've ever done in my life—ohh . . .'' but he decided he had to do it anyway. It was the sort of thing he always did and he was too old to change, he guessed. And just maybe, he thought, that was the story of his life . . .

Frank Belford had used Frost's Bushnells to survey the airfield and he had picked a vintage HU-1D helicopter that was clearly U.S. military surplus from the early days of Viet Nam. "It should handle the job, Frost,'' Belford had pronounced. "Now, all we have to do is steal it.''

As Frost remounted the truck, now, he stood on the running board, staring down at the airfield along the modern highway below them. He shouted back to Belford, "Frank—now we're gonna steal it.''

Frost swung in behind the wheel, the engine

already started, then threw the transmission into second, the grinding of the gears audible in the stillness of the dirt road as the deuce-and-a-half started rolling down the hill and toward the highway. Frost double clutched, upshifting into third to give the vehicle added momentum. Then, as the road steepened, he double clutched again, downshifting to slow the vehicle with the engine compression, the truck slowing as Frost bounced it off the dirt road and onto the highway. Frost upshifted, skipping into third and the tramsmission grinding as he did, the vehicle hanging back with a noticeable power loss, then surging ahead, the engine whining. "Hang on!" Frost shouted, the Swede, Svernbjorg, beside him gripping the doorframe with his vice-like right fist, his mouth twisted down in what Frost interpreted as a mixture of fear and disgust. "You drive as fool!"

Frost looked at the Swede, saying, "Like a fool—you got rotten English."

"You got rotten drive."

Frost glared at the man and laughed. "Right," and Frost wrenched the stick into fourth and started crossing toward the median strip, aiming the massive vintage truck at the chainlink fence ahead of them on the opposite side of the road. Frost wrenched the wheel into a slow left, cutting onto the median then bouncing across it, downshifting into third, then second, then upshifting into third as he hit the opposite lanes. There was a military jeep rolling toward them, some of the Ramon troops visible in it—three men. The man in the front passenger seat was raising an M-16 to fire, and Frost cut the wheel hard right, the deuce-and-half's right front fender impacting against the left front fender of the jeep, upending it, the jeep rolling away, Frost cutting the truck's wheel hard left and guiding around it, then aiming once again toward the far lane.

"Now!" Frost shouted and as he wrenched the wheel left onto the dirt shoulder and toward the fence, in the driver's side mirror he could see the canvas top on the two-and-one-half ton truck ripping down, Belford, Kujinama, Edison, Givens, Fingers Finch and the others with their rifles ready. Beside Frost in the front seat, Svernbjorg shifted the M-60 through the open passenger window and braced it there, opening fire, the staccato of the machinegun as it fired beating a rhythmic tattoo seeming to punctuate the ripping and tearing sound as Frost drove the big truck against the fence, downshifting and punching through it, part of the fencing caught on the bumper and dragging under the vehicle. Frost could hear it, see the sparks as it rubbed against the concrete of the runway when he stuck his head through the window. The wind was blowing hard in the slipstream around the truck as Frost accelerated to fifty crossing the runway toward the helicopter, the guns from his crew of mercenaries in the back firing as Ramon troops started swarming from the hangars and from around the various aircraft the truck passed.

Frost cut the wheel in a hard right, shouting to the Swede, "Duck back—I'm clipping that!"

and Frost punched the deuce-and-a-half into the starboard wing tip of a Soviet jet fighter parked on the runway, then cut the truck away, leaving most of his right front fender attached to the Russian plane. The helicopter loomed ahead of them. Svernbjorg leaned out the passenger window again, firing the machinegun at a pickup truck rolling toward them, the truck lurching to a halt as a burst of the M-60's 7.62mm NATO rounds impacted against the engine block, the engine exploding—the crank case Frost thought—and the hood flying skyward, then the gas tank erupting and the small truck was engulfed in an orange and black and red fireball belching skyward.

Frost kept the truck rolling, spotting a jeep armed with a machinegun in the back racing diagonally across the field toward them. Frost shouted into the back of the truck, "Get that jeep!"

Shooting a glance into the mirror, Frost watched as six of his mercs opened with their assault rifles on the jeep, the machinegun on the jeep cranking toward them and returning fire. Frost's windshield shattered, the truck swerving, then Frost got the truck back under control, glancing into the rearview again as Edison fired one of the M-79s, the whoosh barely audible over the roar of the engine and the gunfire. The jeep bounced once high into the air as the grenade impacted, a fireball erupting from it as Frost turned the wheel into a hard right, the truck almost overturning, the tires and brakes screeching. The helicopter was now less than two hundred yards away.

Frost upshifted into fourth and stepped on the gas pedal, racing the truck toward the chopper, then using the compression to slow it, started double clutching and downshifting, the speed dropping, Frost cutting the wheel into another hard right. The truck half-spun as it began to grind to a halt, Frost cutting down into first and hitting the brakes again, hard, the truck skidding across the runway. As Frost cut the engine and started opening the driver's side door, he glanced again into the mirror—Fingers Finch, Edison, Belford and the others were already piling out of the truck, Belford running toward the chopper and almost diving inside, Givens and Kujinama setting up a rough perimeter defense while Belford would start the chopper blades turning. As Frost hit the runway, Svernbjorg was already out, the M-60 in his massive, gloved hands, the box under the barrel already emptied of one-hundred rounds, the link belts that had been draped across him feeding the big MG as Svernbjorg kept up a steady stream of bursts across the airfield. Ramon troops and some in Cuban uniforms were streaming across the run-way as Frost reached the chopper, climbing aboard, catching at some of the packs of ammunition and explosives Finch and Edison had begun transferring from the deuce-and-a-half into the chopper.

As the last pack came aboard and the men started piling on, Frost barked orders to Edison to get on the twin coaxially mounted M-60s and get them operational if at all possible. Then, slinging his bastardized assault rifle into position, Frost started firing through the open cargo doors, across the airfield toward the Ramon troops and the Cuban "volunteers."

The rotors were already twirling almost lazily overhead, then there was a loud humming sound and the swish of the rotor blades themselves became more audible, the blades seeming almost invisible as they spun more rapidly. Frost looked back to the runways, continuing to fire, bracing himself against the door as Belford shouted something Frost couldn't quite hear. The chopper started to rise, its movements jerky at first as it skimmed slowly over the runway. Then suddenly it was up, the ground disappearing rapidly as Frost continued firing, Edison shouting, Frost turning and seeing him give a thumbs up signal.

Belford was already arcing back over the field, the twin M-60s firing, Svernbjorg standing beside Frost in the open doorway, the M-60 he held firing too. As the Huey helicopter soared over the field, Frost could see the Cubans and the Ramon troops running, the steel jacketed slugs from the M-60s cutting them down in their tracks. Givens and Kujinama were in the doorway as well, firing M-79s, the shotgun-like grenade launchers aimed toward the aircraft still on the field, first one then another of the Soviet fighters exploding.

Frost rammed another stick into the CAR-16, the selector on full-auto, the rest of his mercs in the portside doorway, firing down onto the airfield as well. Belford swept the chopper toward the fenceline, then back, the grenade launchers still firing in one more "bomb" run against the aircraft. There was a large fuel tank visible near a hangar on the far side of the field, a Soviet fighter already taxiing from it. Frost slipped the scope covers on the CAR-16 and fired, full auto. At two hundred yards it took him until the third three round burst—then the gasoline tanks exploded. The air itself around the helicopter seemed to shudder with the concussion. Shouting, his voice hoarse with emotion, tension and some fear, Frost rasped, "Let's get the hell out of here, Frank!" Then, the salt and pepper stubbled smile-frown lines in his face creasing into a smile, Frost lit a Camel in the blue-yellow flame of his battered Zippo. "I think we oughta visit Ramon—I always wanted to play the Palace!"

Chapter Twenty-four

Frost tossed out the first of the red synthetic climbing ropes they would use to rappel from the Huey HU-1D helicopter to the roof of the Presidential Palace. Already, the yard surrounding the vast house and the lake beyond it was alive with gunfire—but most of it aimed toward the trucks pursuing Frost and the others in the stolen helicopter. Frost smiled at the thought, watching the rope uncoil, clipping one of the chrome-plated rings to the rope and getting ready to jump.

Three more ropes smaked downward on Frost's side of the Huey and he looked behind him, six ropes dropping from the port side. Morgan, one of the mercenaries with a long term fighting record in Rhodesia, was staying behind with Frank Belford on the chopper.

Frost gave the command, "Jump!" and almost in unison Frost and the other nine of his mercs started down from the chopper along the ropes. Their feet were spread, the legs slightly angled, the ropes coiled about them as if they were sitting in a chair lift, one hand feeding rope, one hand guiding it and holding it. Frost glanced at his men, watching them, watching the Palace roof as they made their rapid descent. Frost had been the first one out and hit the roof first as well, getting himself untangled from the ropes, slinging the CAR-16 around into position and running to the roof line, seeing and hearing the others behind him.

"Penetration Team!" Frost shouted. "Let's go!" Fingers Finch, Edison, Givens, Kujinama and Svernbjorg knotted together as the four other mercenaries stationed themselves along the roofline. Frost and the five men of the Penetration Team started for the hidden passage leading down into the Palace, Frost searching the rooftop for the louvered wooden shutters third from the end. He stopped, the peeling green paint of the shutters catching his eye. Dropping into a crouch, he tried the shutters—they were closed tight. Standing, Frost lashed out with his right foot, the heel and sole of his combat boot smashing at the joint between the two shutter doors, the wood splintering under the impact.

He kicked again at the shutters, knocking away the remaining pieces of the wood. "Let's go!'' Frost rasped, peering down past the opening for the shutters into the cobwebbed eaves of the Palace, then clambering through, testing the firmness of the floorboards with the butt of the CAR-16, then dropping down and onto the flooring. Sunlight shone under the roofline in tiny streaks as Frost started forward, the stagnant air there stifling. Something scurried over Frost's left foot and he stopped, fumbling the Kel-Lite from his pack, shining it ahead of him on the floor. A mouse, and Frost imagined there were many more. He kept walking, the other five mercenaries behind him in single file. Frost paced himself, trying to gauge the number of yards from the broken shutters, then scanned the interior wall with the flashlight.

"Here," he whispered, stopping, shining the light on a small, almost unnoticeable seam in the wall panels. Kujinama bent forward, studying it. "Got to find the operating mechanism," Frost muttered, sweeping the light away and looking on both sides of the joint then above in the roof and down toward the floor. "Damn," Frost muttered.

"I, ahh—I will do this," Kujinama said resolutely.

Frost stepped back, the Oriental mercenary running the splayed fingers of his hands along the wall panel and over the line of the joint, then stepping back, feet together, head slightly bowed. There was a soft, groaning sound, almost like a yell, Frost thought, and Kujinama's left foot went out, his right hand punching forward at chest level, the fist connecting at the door joint, then streaking back, the panel almost springing inward under his touch.

"Good man," Frost rasped, stepping through into the darkness beyond the panel, then shining the light there. There was a long passage running across the roofline, Frost guessed, and at the far end he could barely discern something looking like the top of a ladder.

Frost walked swiftly forward, toward the ladder, and as the floor boards started creaking under his feet he hugged against the brick that now formed the interior wall to shift his weight to the most solid part of the flooring. The creaking all but stopped and he signalled with the beam of the flashlight for the others, as they followed him, to do the same.

Frost stopped at the ladder, peering down into the darkness, seeing nothing, then shining the Kel-Lite into the well of darkness. The ladder led to a passage that looked to be on a level with the second floor of the Palace as best he could judge.

Frost tested out the ladder rungs, feeling the top one and the one below it creak just under the pressure of his foot. As Kujinama and the others joined him, he swept the light in transverse patterns against the far wall, spotting a brick and masonry chimney, sturdy enough seeming. "Givens," Frost rasped. "Take one of those ropes and hitch it around that chimney—you and the Swede try your weight against it. If the chimney holds, run the rope back down here—we're going down with it."

"Right you are, Captain!" Givens answered smartly, tapping the big red-haired Swede on the shoulder and starting toward the chimney, one of the red climbing ropes already uncoiling. It took less than two minutes, Frost judged, to secure and test the rope against the chimney. They dropped it down, then Frost started after it, using the rope to support his weight as he used the ladder rungs to steady himself.

He dropped the last three feet to the passageway, shining the light across and down its length. He could see the back ends of several fireplaces, then tried remembering what Marina had told him—it was third fireplace he wanted. He started forward, looking over his shoulder as the others of his mercenary crew hit the passageway and started after him.

Frost stopped, shining the light over the rock facing of the third fireplace.

He began counting down the levels of the rocks on the left side as he faced it, found the sixth level, the center of three stones and noticed the masonry around it was gone. A smile crossed the one-eyed man's lips. Snatching the bayonet from his belt, he used the tip to pry against the rock, the rock starting to give, then spring toward him. Like most secret passages of fact, fiction and history—he'd had a professor once that considered history a little of both fact and fiction—this passage was designed to be opened from inside the house, rather than outside. But as the rock sprang into the passageway, there was an almost imperceptible movement of the fire-

213

place backing. Already, the Japanese mercenary Kujinama was pulling on the fireplace from the right side, the center section opening. Frost had no idea who or what might be on the other side. In Marina's day, it had been an unused nursery. "Let's go," Frost snapped diving into the room beyond the fireplace through the opening.

It was dark as he hit the floor, a cardboard packing box starting to slip down on him—Frost caught it with one hand, pushing it back up. He shone the Kel-Lite across the room. There was bright, but dirty floral print paper on the walls, a draped over crib shape in the far corner, and boxes and more boxes stacked around the room. He smiled as he passed an elaborate hobby horse in the center of the floor. Reaching the door, he stopped, listening, but all he heard were the sounds of the others coming up across the room behind him.

If Ramon followed the pattern of the rooms as they had been used in the days of Marina's father, he was a few doors down, in the office. Frost tried the knob on the door—It was locked.

"You, ahh—want me to do the lock?" Kujinama asked.

"No," Frost smiled in the darkness. "I think it's time they realized we were here—come on," and Frost stepped back from the door, then raised his right foot and smashed it against the lock, the door springing loose and cracking as it fell outward. Half jumping over it, Frost hit the hallway—already, the light almost blinding him, there were shouts. The surprise was on.

Chapter Twenty-five

Frost glanced down at the black faced Omega Seamaster 120 on his left wrist, "Right on time," he told himself, then started down the hallway, gunfire and explosions from the Presidential Palace grounds already filling the air, Ramon troops streaming through the courtyard beyond , visible to Frost through the massive windows fronting it.

"Let's go!" Frost shouted, then somebody—he thought it was Fingers Finch—yelled, "Get Ramon!"

Frost started into a dead run toward the third door back—Ramon's office. The plan was rehearsed and rehearsed and rehearsed again. Svernbjorg and Givens and Edison took the head

215

of the stairs, Svernbjorg's M-60 already firing, the other two men with their assault rifles and a M-79 Grenade Launcher. Frost and Kujinama and Fingers Finch raced down the hallway, Ramon troops appearing in a far door—the security room, Frost remembered—and Frost's finger already pumping the assault rifle's trigger, 5.56mm deathpills spitting from the flash deflectored muzzle, the troopers going down.

Kujinama was already at the double office doors, and as Frost wheeled, Kujinama was airborne, at least four feet off the ground, his right leg tucked under him, his elbows pulled against his sides, his face set in something halfway between anxiety and concentration, his left leg streaking out, the foot impacting against the joint of the double doors, the doors bursting inward. Frost and Fingers Finch hit the doorway, Kujinama shouting, a .45 Government Model Colt in his left hand, a knife that looked more like a short sword in his right as he raced between them, streaking toward the desk at the far end of the room.

Frost had picked his men carefully—Kujinama had once been the best assassin in the Orient. The Japanese mercenary seemed to fly from the middle of the room, swan-diving toward the desk, a forty-ish, good looking man, rising from his chair, his right hand going to a flap holster on his hip.

"Get Ramon!" Finch shouted. Kujinama crashed down toward Ernesto Ramon, the desk splitting, then collapsing on itself under the force

216

of Kujinama's body.

Ramon stepped back, going for the pistol in his belt and Frost fired, Kujinama simultaneously lashing outward with the knife, the sword-like edged weapon hacking into Ramon between the neck and left shoulder, Frost's three-round burst pumping into the Castro puppet dictator's chest and neck, the body seeming to explode in blood as it toppled backward. Frost wheeled, hearing Finch's rifle discharging—two men were at the far right hand side of the room, standing by a wall map, one of the men already going down under Finch's assault rifle fire, a gun crumpling from his left hand, the second man just staring. Frost recognized the insignia of a Cuban General. He started walking across the room toward the man, Kujinama muttering something Frost assumed was in Japanese as the knife sliced menacingly through the air, Finch holding his left hand, cursing, "That sucker shot me. Almost cut off my sixth finger and made me damned normal!"

Frost started to laugh, stopping in front of the Cuban General. A name tag read "Martin" which Frost guessed was pronounced "Marteen". The man's armpits were staining with sweat, beads of perspiration pouring from his forehead. Frost poked the muzzle of the CAR-16 at the Cuban, the flash deflector touching the man's nose. Finch held his assault rifle in a guard position, a smile on his face as Frost kept laughing. Kujinama was still swinging the knife through the air, letting it roll over his hands, soar upward, then catching it to repeat the routine.

"You have one option, General—tell the volunteers to hang it up, lay down their arms and they can go home unmolested. Otherwise, Fingers here will kneecap you, I'll blow away the front of your nose and Kujinama will disembowel you—all at once."

"Yo no—"

"Bullshit," Frost told him. "If you don't speak English now you're in big trouble. Your move."

"You are the one with the eyepatch—Frost."

"Believe it," Frost smiled, pushing the flash deflector closer to the man's nose.

"Si—yo creo—yes," the man stammered. "There is a radio, I—"

"Kujinama and Finch will take you to it—and be quick about it."

As the Cuban Communist started trailing across the office floor and the oriental rug there, he turned, looking at Frost, saying nothing. Frost nodded, saying, "I give you my word—both ways. You co-operate and any man that harms you or your men answers to me."

The General nodded, started to salute then apparently thought better of it. Frost shook his head, walking slowly toward the windows beyond the bloody hulk that had been Ramon. He looked down into the courtyard. Even though the Cuban General could not yet have signalled his men to lay down their arms, the fighting was already begining to slow. Parachutes filled the sky around the Presidential Palace as the mass jump by Commacho's forces continued. Frost still had no idea who Commacho knew in Washington to get the planes. Commacho's troops were moving slowly through the courtyard, and already the defenders of the Palace were starting to lay down their arms, most of the resistance fading.

Frost lit a Camel in the blue-yellow flame of his Zippo—there was nothing but shouting now coming from the hall. Now all he had to do, he realized, to collect his one hundred thousand dollars, was to settle things up with Adolpho Commacho—the commanding General who wanted him dead.

Chapter Twenty-six

By six P.M., the sun starting to slightly fade, the official Ramon Government radio had signalled surrender, Commacho's forces dominated the capital and most of the interior from their overland sweep—the fighting had largely stopped except for scattered pockets of resistance. And Frost had kept his word to the Cuban General—none of the Cuban volunteers who had surrendered had been shot.

By the next morning most of the Cubans had been captured or surrendered and the Commacho forces were consolidating their positions. Marina was arriving by helicopter, landing in the courtyard—and so was Adolpho Commacho.

Frost watched as the machine settled onto the

burnt out and neglected grass—he remembered it being as springy as a rich man's carpet and as green as a shamrock. Frost stood, leaning against a support pillar, beside the low steps leading down into the courtyard. Marina ran from the chopper toward him, up the steps and into his arms. "Hank—you have won!"

"You have won, kid," Frost smiled, kissing her lightly then on the lips, "Me—I've just worked myself out of a job."

"I want you to stay—always, carino!"

He bent and kissed her forehead, then gently half shoved her aside as he started down the low steps, saying to her," You couldn't have me stay after this," and he stopped at the base of the steps, looking across the courtyard toward the helicopter and young, swarthy Adolpho Commacho, standing there, his eyes hard.

Frost had welcomed the chance of a shower in the Presidential Palace the previous night, changed from his fatigues to the slacks from a white suit Ramon had owned—they were a good fit. The white shirt he'd also borrowed from the dead man was opened half to his waist, the grey and black hairs on his chest dripping sweat despite the hour. The Metalifed Browning High Power was jammed into his trouser belt. "Adolpho—what now?"

"It is time, Frost."

"I respected your uncle, called him friend. He would have understood I derailed his train to save the man he served—Marina's father."

"You crawl, you beg!" the young Adolpho sneered.

Frost was suddenly very tired—of a lot of things. "You are full of shit," he answered calmly.

"My jacket," the man shouted back, edging away from the helicopter, its rotor blades still swishing lazily through the humid air.

"Feel free, pal," Frost told the man.

Adolpho Commacho undid the zipper of the fatigue jacket he wore, the jacket dripping, Frost thought, with brass denoting his rank as General.

He wore a grey shirt, the armpits stained with sweat. Methodically, the man rolled up the sleeves of his shirt, then slowly, nodding to Frost who nodded back, dropped the pistol belt to the ground, slipping the ornately engraved, pearl handled Smith & Wesson revolver he carried into his trouser band.

"Soy—I am ready!"

"Aren't you gonna shout, hey, toro or something?"

"Marina will drop a handkerchief."

"Will a tissue do if she doesn't have a hand-kerchief?"

"Silence!"

"Bite it!"

Frost glanced to Marina. Her lips were moving but no words coming. "Somebody get her back up on the steps," Frost rasped to the men standing around her. Then, to Adolpho Commacho, Frost shouted, "You go for your gun when you feel it is right. I bear you no malice, no ill will—you are a fool to do this. We could both die."

222

"There is no shame in that."

"You know," Frost smiled, "this whole Macho thing is indicative of a pile of hangups, Adolpho."

"Silence!" And Adolpho's right hand flashed toward the pearl butt of the Smith revolver, Frost's right hand wrapping around the checkered rubber Pachmayr grips on the Metalifed 9mm pistol in his belt, the muzzle clearing his trouser band as his right thumb jerked back on the hammer. His mind filled with visions of all the western gunfight movies he'd seen, his left leg flashing out, his right knee bending as he dodged down and left, Commacho's revolver firing, the big bore centerfire belching flame and Frost's right shoulder suddenly burning, Frost's right hand loosing the High Power, his left snatching for it and pulling the trigger.

Frost's first shot impacted against the pavement between Commacho's feet, and as Commacho brought his revolver down out of recoil—he was firing one-handed—Frost settled his grip on the High Power and fired twice again, both rounds impacting into Commacho's center of mass. The revolver discharged into the ground as Adolpho doubled forward and dropped, dead before he hit the ground.

Frost stood up, the Browning hanging loosely in his left hand, his right shoulder aching and streaming blood. He turned to look at Marina. Her eyes were wide, the darkness of them glassy looking.

223

Fumbling up the safety on the Browning and jamming the gun in his belt, he shrugged and his shoulder hurt as he did, and all he said was, "I was right—you couldn't have me stay after this." He was starting to pass out, more from the shock of the heavy caliber slug than loss of blood, and as his knees buckled, Frost saw her start to run down the steps toward him. He heard her whisper as he lay back with his head in her blue jeaned lap, "Si," and then, so softly Frost knew only he could hear it, "Carino." In Spanish, it meant darling, and more.

He didn't pass out and as Marina walked beside him while two of his mercenaries helped him into the Palace, a medic was already tending the arm. As they walked, Frost decided two things. Maybe with the hundred thousand he would learn to fly, at least a couple of lessons. The second thing was that once he boarded the plane and kissed Marina good-bye it would be forever—or at least until the next time.